Praise for Kate Hoffmann's The Mighty Quinns

"[Kate] Hoffmann always brings a strong story to the table with The Mighty Quinns, and this is one of her best."

—*RT Book Reviews* on *The Mighty Quinns: Eli*

"[Hoffmann's] characters are well written and real. *The Mighty Quinns: Eli* is a recommended read for lovers of the Quinn family, lovers of the outdoors and lovers of a sensitive man."

—*Harlequin Junkie*

"Hoffmann always does a great job creating different stories for the members of the Quinn clan."

—*RT Book Reviews* on *The Mighty Quinns: Rogan*

"A winning combination of exciting adventure and romance... This is a sweet and sexy read that kept me entertained from start to finish."

—*Harlequin Junkie* on *The Mighty Quinns: Malcolm*

"As usual, Hoffmann has written a light yet compelling tale with just enough angst and long-term background story to provide momentum for the next member of the Quinn family we are most certainly going to meet."

—*RT Book Reviews* on *The Mighty Quinns: Ryan*

Dear Reader,

I've been writing for the Harlequin Blaze line for about as long as the imprint has been in existence. And the Mighty Quinns have been a part of my writing life for fifteen years and thirty-four stories!

In this final book of my "Black Sheep" series of the Mighty Quinns, I've taken on an unusual challenge—a virgin heroine and a hero with no past. Working with quirky characters can be a lot of fun and opens new doors when it comes to the romantic relationship.

I hope you enjoy Mac and Emma's story as much as I enjoyed writing it.

Happy reading,

Kate Hoffmann

Kate Hoffmann

The Mighty Quinns: Mac

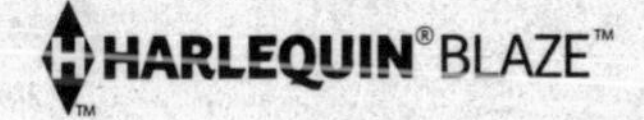

ISBN-13: 978-0-373-79871-1

The Mighty Quinns: Mac

This edition published by arrangement with Harlequin Books S.A.

For questions and comments about the quality of this book, please contact us at CustomerService@Harlequin.com.

Printed in U.S.A.

Kate Hoffmann celebrated her twentieth anniversary as a Harlequin author in August 2013. She has published over eighty books, novellas and short stories for Harlequin Temptation and Harlequin Blaze. She spent time as a music teacher, a retail assistant and an advertising exec before she settled into a career as a full-time writer. Her other interests include genealogy, musical theater and vegan cooking. She lives in southeastern Wisconsin with her two cats, Winnie and Gracie.

Books by Kate Hoffmann

HARLEQUIN BLAZE

The Mighty Quinns

The Mighty Quinns: Dermot
The Mighty Quinns: Kieran
The Mighty Quinns: Cameron
The Mighty Quinns: Ronan
The Mighty Quinns: Logan
The Mighty Quinns: Jack
The Mighty Quinns: Rourke
The Mighty Quinns: Dex
The Mighty Quinns: Malcolm
The Mighty Quinns: Rogan
The Mighty Quinns: Ryan
The Mighty Quinns: Eli
The Mighty Quinns: Devin

To Birgit Davis-Todd, who first suggested I write about the Quinns.

Prologue

"WHAT'S YOUR NAME, SON?"

Lukas sat on the edge of the gurney, his gaze darting around the exam room. He was trapped by a pale green curtain on three sides, and he fought the impulse to run. It would only make him look more suspicious and he was unsure of what was waiting on the other side.

The police officer pulled up a stool and sat down, resting his hand on Luke's knee. "Do you know where your parents are? They were with you ten days ago when you checked into the motel. What happened?"

Tears welled in the corners of his eyes. How long had it been? He'd lost count of the days since the fight. It had been a particularly violent argument between his mother and father, and, as usual, he'd locked himself in the bathroom, covering his ears against the bitter words they'd flung at each other.

But this fight had been different. The next morning, when he'd woken up, they were gone. He'd found himself alone, his meager belongings scattered around the motel room. He'd waited, certain they'd return for him. As the days passed and he'd been forced to search the trash cans for food, Luke realized that he was twelve years old and he was on his own.

"Do you have any relatives we can call?" the officer asked.

It had always been just the three of them, as long as he could remember. They'd moved around a lot, sometimes staying in motels for weeks on end, other times settling into a house or an apartment when his father found work. Luke would enroll in school and life would seem almost normal.

Then, something would happen and they'd be off again, slipping away in the dark of night, leaving behind anything that couldn't fit in the car.

He couldn't remember when life wasn't like this, when his father wasn't angry and abusive and when his mother wasn't terrified. They were running from something—or someone—dangerous. Whoever or whatever it was, it was always just a few steps behind them.

"I—I'm not sure where they are," Luke murmured.

He knew just one truth. They were gone and he was all alone in the world—all alone against some invisible threat that still stalked him. They'd left St. Louis two days ago, on the run again. He wasn't even sure where they were now. Colorado? Utah? They'd been headed to Oregon, but that's all he'd been told.

"Where do you live?"

"I can't remember," he insisted.

"Son, I don't think—"

"I don't know," Luke said. "Can I leave now?"

"No, you can't leave. We need to find a relative," the officer said, "or you're going to have to go into the foster care system. You don't want to do that, do you?"

In truth, the option sounded good to him. He'd be safe, hidden among strangers. Luke wasn't sure how long he'd be able to survive on his own. He had no money, nowhere to sleep, nothing to eat. "It's okay," he said. "You can send me there."

"No relatives? No one who might want to take you in?"

Luke shook his head, then slipped off the edge of the gurney. "I'm hungry. Can I get something to eat?"

The officer stood up. "Let me see what I can find," he murmured.

Luke circled the gurney and found a dark corner where he could think. Up until a few weeks ago, he'd been Lukas Parrish. But since leaving St. Louis he was Lukas MacKenzie. "M-A-C-capital-K-E-N-Z-I-E," he murmured to himself. His father had made him spell it over and over again until it came naturally. There had been other names in other places. He had no idea which one to use. He knew that Parrish wasn't his real last name, either. Before Parrish it had been Cartwright, and before that, Phillips. If he thought about it hard enough, he could come up with ten or fifteen different names. Since MacKenzie was the last name his father had told him to use, that was the name he'd given the police.

Pulling his knees up to his chest, he wrapped his arms over his head, wrapping his body into a tight ball. The tears stung his eyes and Luke finally surrendered to his fears. A string of curses burst from his lips and he felt a surge of anger toward his parents. How could they do this to him?

This was all his fault. He should have been brave and convinced his mother to leave his father. He should have kept her safe. They could have made a good life for themselves. But his father was a selfish, obsessive man. He hadn't been happy unless he controlled every facet of his family's lives. He'd always said it was for their safety, but Luke knew better. His father would never have let his mother go.

He saw a policewoman approach and he avoided her gaze, knowing there would be more questions.

"How are you doing, Luke?" she asked in a kind voice.

"Not so good," Luke murmured. "Am I going to foster care soon?"

She pulled something out of her pocket and held it out to him. It was the little tin box of treasures that he kept with him. Luke wasn't sure where the box had come from, but he'd always had it. No matter where they moved, his mother helped him find a proper hiding place for it, a spot that his father wouldn't find. Luke wasn't sure why it meant so much them. He assumed that the contents of the box must be important.

"Is this yours?" the officer asked.

Luke nodded and he took the box from her outstretched hand. "Can you find a photo of your mother in there?"

Luke sorted through it and held up a shot of the two of them together taken in a photo booth at a seaside amusement park. He'd been young, but he remembered that day—the warm sand and the salty sea breeze. The gulls that swooped down from the sky to finish the remains of Luke's and his mother's sandwiches.

"This is her?" the policewoman asked.

Luke nodded.

"Do you have a picture of your father?"

"He doesn't like photos."

She held out a small wallet-sized album. "What about these people? They look older. Are they your grandparents?"

He shook his head. "I'm not sure who they are."

"And these wedding bands? And this watch? Who does this belong to?"

Luke shrugged. "They've always been in the box. I don't know."

The rest of the treasures were things he'd added—a seashell, a piece of pink quartz, an old Indian head nickel. Had his father known of the box, the contents would have been pawned long ago.

"We're going to make a copy of this photo and see if we can track down your parents," she said. "And if you remember anything else, you give me a call, all right?" She handed him a business card. "That's my home number."

"I don't think they want me," he said. Tears filled his eyes and spilled out onto his cheeks. Though he tried to stop them by sheer force of will, nothing he thought or did seemed to control his grief. She rubbed his back until he stopped crying, then handed him a wad of tissues.

"I can't believe that's true," she said.

Maybe he was wrong. But until he was sure, he'd follow his father's rules. The rules would keep him safe. His name was Luke MacKenzie. But his friends called him Mac.

1

"WHO ARE YOU? Where's Buddy? I need to talk to Buddy. When will he be back?"

Luke MacKenzie grabbed a rag from the floor of the airplane hangar and wiped the grease from his hands. As he approached the counter, he studied the woman who had burst through the door just a few seconds before.

Her dark hair was windblown and the color was high on her cheeks. His gaze dropped to her lush lips and perfect white teeth. Her expression, though tense with anger, did nothing to diminish her natural beauty. In truth, he hadn't met anyone quite so beautiful in a very long time.

Mac grinned lazily and walked up to the counter. "Which one of those questions would you like me to answer first?" he asked, leaning closer to her.

Her scowl deepened. "Where's Buddy?"

"He's in the hospital having his hip replaced."

The news seemed to take her by surprise and he detected a slight blush creeping up her cheeks. "Oh," she murmured. "He did tell me that. When is he going to be back?"

"About three weeks," he said. "Maybe a month."

"And who are you?"

"Luke MacKenzie," he said. "They call me Mac." He wiped his hand on his jeans and held it out. To his surprise, she took and shook it firmly. Mac held on for a few moments longer, enjoying the feel of her slender fingers resting in his palm.

"Mr. MacKenzie, I—"

"Just Mac," he insisted, giving her hand another squeeze.

She straightened her spine and met his gaze, then slowly tugged her hand from his. "Well, Mr. Just Mac, let me give you the 411 because obviously Buddy didn't fill you in before he left. The next time Charlie Clemmons shows up and wants you to haul that ridiculous Marry Me, Emma banner all over the sky, you're supposed to tell him no!"

"And your name is..."

"Emma," she murmured. "Emma Bryant."

"Well, Marry-Me Emma, Buddy might be able to turn down two hundred dollars for an airborne marriage proposal, but I don't have that luxury. As long as Charlie's money is green, I'm gonna take the job."

"But you don't understand. This has become an obsession with Charlie. And I'm not going to marry him. Not now. Not ever. So he can waste all the money he wants but I'm not going to change my mind."

"Maybe he's in love," Mac suggested.

"And maybe he's completely insane," she countered.

"Why don't you want to marry him?"

"Haven't you been listening? He's insane. He just won't let go. It's not healthy."

"Is there another reason you don't want to marry him? Maybe there's someone else?"

She gasped, then fixed him with a glare that could melt steel. "That is none of your business! And if I were you, I wouldn't listen to town gossip."

"There's gossip? I'm afraid I'm out of the loop. I've got a few minutes. Why don't you fill me in? Can I get you something cold to drink? I've got a Yoo-hoo back in the fridge."

She looked at him as if he'd just asked her to strip naked and join him in a round of "The Hokey Pokey." "I'm sure you think you're charming, and I'm sure that charm works on a certain element of society, but it's not going to work on me."

"You didn't answer my question," he said.

"You didn't ask me a question," she said.

"Sure I did. I asked if there was someone else. A boyfriend or a fiancé? I could see how a stray marriage proposal might be problematic in that situation."

She really was a beautiful woman, Mac mused. Her short dark hair curled gently around her pretty face, enhancing wide eyes and a lush mouth that had been made to be kissed. She also had thick lashes that ringed her brilliant green eyes—eyes that seemed to see right into his soul.

"Just don't fly any more of his banners," she warned. She spun on her heel and started for the door, but he called her name and she stopped and slowly faced him.

"You know, the fastest way to get rid of the old guy is to take up with a new guy."

"You think I don't know that? When you live in a small town like San Coronado, decent men are in short supply. Believe me, I've been looking."

"Maybe you haven't been looking hard enough," Mac suggested.

She strode toward the door, but before she had a chance to pull it open, he spoke.

"You could go out with me," Mac said. "I'm new in town, and I haven't met many people. It would be nice to have someone show me around." He'd issued the request more as an experiment than an actual invitation. And as an excuse to keep her in the shop just a little bit longer.

He found her quite fascinating, this stunningly beautiful girl who couldn't seem to find a man. But now that he'd made the invitation, he wanted her to accept. "Let me get you that Yoo-hoo and we can talk over the particulars. Give me a chance to apologize for the whole banner problem."

She stared at him for a long moment. "You're asking me out? On a date?"

"Yes," he said.

"We just met. And I don't think I like you."

"'Tis one thing to be tempted," he murmured. "Another to fall."

"Do you really believe a little Shakespeare is going to make me swoon for you?"

"Swoon? What does that mean?"

"Look it up," she said.

"I left my dictionary in my other toolbox," he teased. "Do you like Shakespeare?"

"He's only the greatest writer who ever lived."

"So where do you come down in the authorship issue? Are you a Stratfordian or an Oxfordian?" Clearly his question had taken her by surprise. He also noticed a bit of interest in her expression. "I just finished a new book on the subject."

"The Weight of the Words?" Emma asked. "I loved that book."

"We should get together and discuss it," he said.

Emma opened her mouth, then frowned, shaking her head. "Just don't do it again," she warned. With that, she walked out of the hangar and into the bright sunshine of the October day.

"Do what again?" Mac shouted. "Ask you out on a date? Or fly that banner?"

He strolled over to the door and stared out, hoping to catch one last glimpse of her. But she'd already hopped in her car and started to race the battered Volvo station wagon down the airstrip road, a cloud of dust trailing behind it.

J. J. Jones, Buddy's mechanic, strolled around the corner of the hangar wall and handed an old hydraulic pump to Mac. "Was that Emma Bryant?"

"Yeah," Mac said.

"I told you not to fly that banner," J.J. said.

"What do you know about her?" he asked.

"Know about her?" He grabbed the pump from Mac's hand. "We went to school together. She's the same age as I am. Twenty-seven. She's the town librarian. Her dad died when she was young and her mom passed away about three years ago after a long illness. Emma was devoted to her. Cared for her at home for almost four years."

"If she's such a saint, why do people gossip about her?" he asked.

J.J. gave him an uneasy look. "What do you mean?"

"She asked if I'd heard the gossip around town about her. What gossip?"

"Listen, I don't like tellin' tales. My mama said if I keep my mouth shut and my hands clean I'd go far in life. I always follow my mama's advice."

"Come on. If it's something everyone around town knows, why can't you spill?" Mac prodded. "Is she crazy? Like bunny-boiler crazy?"

J.J. shook his head. "She's real nice. She's one of the nicest people I've ever met. Always very generous with her time. Everyone loves her. Everyone."

"So she's perfect?"

He nodded. "As close to perfect as you're going to get," J.J. said. "You won't catch me saying anything bad about her."

Mac sighed. "You think she'd go out with me?" he asked.

"I doubt you'd be her type," J.J. said.

"She's picky, then," he said.

"She's careful," J.J. countered.

Mac frowned. What did that mean? *Careful?* She was a twenty-seven-year-old single woman. If she was looking for love, she'd have to take some risks to find it. "So she hangs out at the library?"

J.J. grabbed the pump. "I gotta get back to work. That pump on your plane is shot. We should probably replace both of them while we're at it. Want me to order two?"

"No, just get me one," Mac murmured. "And find me a decent price."

"I will," J.J. said.

Mac's gaze was drawn back to the road where Emma Bryant had disappeared. This was a strange feeling, Mac mused. It wasn't often that he found himself genuinely intrigued by a woman. His reactions to the female gender came in one of two varieties—*she's hot and I'd like to take her to bed*...or, *no, thank you.* But this was something very different.

"Emma Bryant," he murmured to himself as he walked back inside. Marry-Me Emma. If he took the proposal sign up again tomorrow morning, he could be assured that she'd stop by again and register her opinion.

"I THINK HE asked me out." Emma paused, then shook her head. "Or maybe I just imagined it. Everything just happened so quickly. The conversation jumped around so much I could barely keep up. But I'm pretty sure there was an invitation in there."

"What did you say?"

"I can't remember." Emma turned to her best friend, Trisha Kelling, and shrugged. "I wish I could rewind the whole thing and listen to it again."

"Wait," Trisha said. "Pull over."

"What?"

"Just pull over. We need your full concentration."

Emma did as she was instructed, steering the station wagon to the edge of the dusty road. She threw it into Park and faced her friend, taking a deep breath.

"What did he look like?" Trish asked.

"Cute. No, handsome. Really sexy. Dark hair, pale blue eyes. You know like blue denim that has been faded by the sun."

"Oh, God, I love that kind of blue," Trisha said. "What else?"

"Straight nose. Not too big. Just right. Nice teeth. And a really nice body, at least, what I was able to see of it."

"What about the goods?" she said. "Did you check that out?"

"No! Why would I check out his…crotch?"

"All right. Was he charming or just kind of full of himself?"

"A little bit of both. But I think he might have been teasing me. He was clever. He seemed really smart. He quoted Shakespeare at me."

"Really? What did he say?"

Trish was an English teacher at the high school and knew her Shakespeare. Emma searched her memory for the phrase, but she couldn't recall the exact words—a sign that Luke MacKenzie had really flustered her. "Something about being tempted and then falling."

"'Tis one thing to be tempted? Another thing to fall?"

"Yes! That's it. *As You Like It*?"

"I should remember where it comes from and don't you dare tell anyone that I don't." Trish pulled out her phone and punched in the quote. "*Measure For Measure*. What do you think he meant?"

"I'm not sure." Emma rubbed her face with her hands. "After that he started talking about the authorship controversy, the Oxfordians versus the Stratfordians. It was as if he knew I was fascinated with the subject and he was tempting me."

"'Tis one thing to be tempted…" Trisha said.

Emma smiled. "This could be it. He could be the one. It makes sense, doesn't it?"

"He's handsome and sexy. He appears to have a brain. And an abundance of charm."

"And he's only going to be in town for a short time. Six weeks at the most. That's perfect," Emma said. "I can't believe I'm finally going to rid myself of this awful virginity. I'll have sex with this man and it will finally be done."

Emma drew a deep breath and let it out slowly. She'd never intended to remain a virgin for this long. It had just happened. Each year had passed without a potential lover in sight and before she knew it, she'd ended up here, more than halfway to thirty and still as chaste as a nun.

"I shouldn't have walked out," Emma said. "I should have flirted with him."

"You could always go back," Trish suggested.

"Under what pretense?"

"An apology for being such a bitch?"

"I *was* a bitch. I just couldn't believe he was serious. A guy like that…and me. Marian the Librarian."

"You could take him a book!" Trisha said. "You know he reads Shakespeare. If he likes Whitman, then he's the ultimate sex machine."

"Whitman? No, that would seem so…obvious. And a little desperate."

"But you are desperate," Trish said. "Maybe it would

be best to just admit that right at the top. There is something sexy about a woman desperate to copulate."

"Copulate?"

"My mother always taught me to use the proper terms for sex."

"Alice Pettit told me to keep my knees together and my feet on the floor," Emma said. "Marliss Franks warned me that naughty girls burn in hell and Reverend Kopitsky said that my body is sacred and my virtue worth more than gold. It really didn't matter, though. Once I got that stupid brace, the boys stayed away."

Her teenage years had been lonely at best. She'd been diagnosed with scoliosis at age thirteen and had worn a back brace through most of high school. Burdened also with massive orthodontia and a bad case of acne, she hadn't been the most attractive option for a prom date. Just months after the brace came off, her mother had been diagnosed with cancer and Emma's attention had turned to nursing her. There'd never been time to date, and without dating—and living in a small town—sex had become an unreachable goal. Now, after all these years of chastity, she felt vulnerable, unprepared for a relationship. She had no idea how to talk to boys or flirt. She still felt like the girl with the back brace and the pimples.

She'd always taken solace in her studies, graduating at the top of her high school class. After high school came college and grad school. She'd lived at home, for both convenience and cost, and so she could watch over her mother's care.

Four years ago, she'd finished her masters in information sciences and been offered the head librarian's job at the small library in town. Though she'd always dreamed about leaving town and starting life somewhere new, Emma stayed to see her mother though the last stages of her illness.

The people of San Coronado had always stood behind her and her mother, Elaine. Elaine had been a beloved kindergarten teacher at the local school and everyone had known her. During her illness, there'd been lots of volunteers who'd arranged fund-raisers—spaghetti dinners and bake sales and benefit concerts—all to help with her mother's medical costs. A prayer circle had spent two hours a week praying for her recovery. How could Emma refuse the job and a chance to return something to the community that had given her mother so much love and attention?

So she'd thrown herself into her work, completely updating the library's catalog system, rearranging the floor plan and adding new programs for children and seniors. And though her mother had urged her to get out and socialize, it was easier to just work into the late hours and then flop into bed when she got home.

She'd had dreams once. She and her mother had always talked about traveling together, taking the summer to see exotic places. They'd pored over travel books and planned itineraries, keeping their notes in leather-bound journals.

New Zealand, Indonesia, Portugal, Finland, Costa Rica. Lists of things to see and do, places to eat. Even during the worst of her mother's illness, they'd kept at it, as if the work held some magic cure.

And once it was clear there would be no cure, her mother made her promise that she'd find a way to go on her own. She'd save her money and buy a ticket to one of the places that had fascinated them both.

As for her lack of social life, that had really been her own fault. After her mother's death, she'd given herself the chance to grieve. It had been easy to shut herself in the house and avoid people. The more time that passed, the more overwhelming getting back out there became. She pushed aside thoughts of a social life to focus entirely on a rigorous work schedule. But now, she felt as if the world had passed her by.

There were a few available men left in town and at least one of them was interested. But trying to start a relationship underneath a microscope was daunting. Everyone seemed a bit too invested in her happily-ever-after.

"I know how difficult it's been on you," Trish said.

"I'm not complaining," she said, shaking her head. "I'm a lucky woman. I have a wonderful job and a wonderful best friend. I don't need anything else."

"Yes, you do!" Trish cried. "You need to feed your soul and your heart. You need passion in your life. And a few really good orgasms. I think this Mac guy is the answer to all your problems."

"Let's say I do decide that I want to pursue something...carnal with Mac," Emma said. "I have to be ready to do it. I mean, it could happen quickly, right? Sometimes, the passion is so overwhelming you just can't help yourself."

"Sometimes," Trisha agreed.

"So, I should buy some sexy underwear and do the whole wax thing. And a mani and a pedi. I'll get my hair cut, too, so I don't look like a demented bear the morning after. Oh, and I have to be ready to provide breakfast if he stays the night. I'll have to plan a menu. And I probably should brush up on…you know…sex."

"How are you going to do that?"

"We have a whole section of books in the library in our self-help section. They're quite informative. I expect he's going to be good at it, so I'd like to return the favor."

"There is a possibility that you might be overanalyzing this," Trish said. "I'll be honest with you, once you start taking off your clothes, there's not a lot of time to think."

"Great advice," Emma murmured. She reached out and restarted the car, then pulled it back out onto the road. She gripped the wheel with white-knuckled fingers, her mind spinning with the possibility that her long ordeal might be over soon.

There were some women who chose to be virgins until they married. But Emma knew she'd never marry. And sex was something that she wanted to experience, a simple human need that had to be satisfied.

"There is another option," Trisha said. "I was reading an article a couple weeks ago about a brothel in Nevada that had men on the menu. You could always pay for it. For the right price, I bet Joey would consider it."

"You're offering up your husband?" Emma asked.

"Not to you," Trish said. "Besides, you're looking for a perfect male specimen, not a guy with a furry chest and the body of a teddy bear." She shrugged. "What can I say? I find the man incredibly sexy. And he's always been so enthusiastic in the sack. And he's got the goods."

"Thank you for your generous offer, but I'm going to have to refuse. But I will buy you lunch."

As they drove toward town, past pastures and vast irrigated fields, the windows of the car open to the afternoon breeze, Emma felt happy, as if the future had suddenly opened up in front of her. There weren't many days when she didn't think about the lack of passion and adventure in her life. But today, she was different. There was an excitement that burned inside her…a delicious anticipation that her life was about to change.

MAC STARED UP at the facade of the San Coronado Public Library. A bronze plaque beside the door designated the neoclassical building as an Andrew Carnegie library, one of over a thousand built by the wealthy industrialist in the early part of the twentieth century in small towns all over the US.

Though he'd been asking J.J. about Emma since he'd met her the day before yesterday, the most he'd been able to pull out of the other man was that she was the town librarian and that everyone loved her. He didn't really need much more. She'd most likely be inside and when she saw him, they'd talk.

He smoothed his hand through his hair, then took the steps two at a time. As he opened the front door, two younger boys slipped inside before him and he noticed a crowd gathered in the lobby. Mac had expected a quiet interior where people spoke in hushed tones. But instead, the place was bustling with noise and activity.

Scattered about was a display of model cars and trucks, made from the kits he'd enjoyed as a kid. Mac smiled as he wandered around the room, remembering the times he'd spent meticulously piecing each model together, then painting it. It was one of the after-school activities at the local Boys and Girls Club. After the disappearance of his parents, he'd been put into the foster care program and had spent most afternoons at the club, finishing his homework and working on models with a few friends.

The models had kept him off the streets and out of the gangs. And when he finished one, he'd gather up the money he made on his paper route and buy another. They'd been stacked from floor to ceiling in their boxes, tucked inside his closet.

On the day he'd turned eighteen, he'd packed his bags and walked away from foster care, leaving the cars and the memories of his boyhood behind. In a single day, he'd become a man, wholly responsible for his own life. He could no longer busy himself with childish things.

He'd found a job, a cheap room at a local boardinghouse and had begun his life, scraping together money for flying lessons and a few classes on engine repair. He taught himself to weld and though he couldn't afford college, he'd gotten a library card and begun to educate himself.

"It's a '57 Chevy! Not a '56. See?"

He glanced down at a young boy who was pointing at a model. "You're right. You can tell by the trim. But I prefer the '56. There's just something about it. The softer fin or the trim piece that curves down."

The little boy smiled. "I prefer it, too."

"We both have excellent taste." Mac winked at him,

then moved on through the crowd to the circulation desk. He scanned the counter for Emma's pretty face, but didn't find her. He decided to get a library card first and make a casual inquiry about Emma at the same time.

"I'd like to get a library card," he said to the woman at the front desk.

"Do you have identification?"

"I do, but it doesn't have my local address on it."

"Do you have a utility bill or something to prove you're a resident of San Coronado?"

"I don't," he said.

"Anyone who could vouch for you?"

"Yes. Emma Bryant could. I understand she works here."

The woman smiled. "She does."

"Is she working today?"

"Yes, she's downstairs in our archives cataloguing some items that were bequeathed to the library last week."

Mac took the form. "I'll just go get her signature and be right back."

"Down the hall and through the door on the right, then down the stairs," the librarian said.

As he followed the directions, Mac felt an odd rush of anticipation. Women had always been a commodity in his life. Though he appreciated each for their individual attributes, Mac found it difficult to make any long-lasting connections.

When the time was right, he made sure he was the one who walked away first. There had been a few women who had been difficult to leave, but he could never truly believe they had any kind of future together. Without trust, any deeper emotions were impossible.

He already knew ending things with Emma would be painful. He was already obsessed with her. She was unique, intriguing, wildly sexy and smart—a deadly combination. It would take a careful approach to charm her, a disciplined plan to hold her and every ounce of his determination to leave her.

The basement of the library was dark and musty and he followed the sound of music through the rows of shelves and storage cabinets. Finally, he reached a central area of tables illuminated by florescent lights. Mac stood in the shadows and observed her for a moment, taking in the scene in greater detail.

An old gramophone sat on one end of the table and it played a classical piece that sounded like a Mozart string quartet. Emma was seated with her back to him, her legs tucked up beneath her, her attention fixed on a paper she was reading.

The dark waves of her hair fell around her face and his fingers twitched as he imagined how it would feel to smooth a curl from her temple and tuck it behind her ear. He'd touched her once, when he'd held her hand, but it hadn't been enough.

He'd known a lot of women whom he'd considered beautiful, Mac mused. But now, he realized that they hadn't really been beautiful at all. They'd made themselves up to reflect what society considered beautiful—blond hair, full lips, high cheekbones, striking eyes.

As he looked at Emma, he saw something simpler, much more pure. There was no need for paint or artifice. It was all there in its natural form. A shiver skittered through his body and his breath caught in his throat.

Emma jumped, then turned around in her chair to find him watching her. She scrambled to her feet, dropping the letter on the table and struggling with the chair. "Wha-what are you doing here?"

"I didn't mean to frighten you," Mac said.

"You did! Why are you here?"

He held up the application for a library card. "I need you to sign this. I wanted to get a card but I don't have the proper identification with me. If you vouch for me, they'll give me one."

"But I don't know you."

He grinned. "Sure you do. I'm the guy who's working for Buddy while he recovers from his surgery."

"And that's all I know. That's not enough to get you a library card. Where do you live?"

"Right now, I'm staying out at the hangar. But I've been trying to find a place in town." That wasn't exactly the truth, but it sounded good. He had a cot, a bathroom and a makeshift kitchen at the hangar. It was rent-free and enough to meet his needs.

"But where do you come from? Where do you live when you're not here?"

Mac wished that he had a better story to tell her, but he'd accepted the reality of his life long ago. "The last time I had a permanent address was the day before my eighteenth birthday. That was nearly ten years ago. I suppose I could give you that address."

"Where was that?"

"Boulder, Colorado. It's where my foster parents

live. At least it was. I haven't talked to them since I left, so they might have moved."

She gave him a grudging smile, then held out her hand. Emma grabbed the paper and signed the bottom. "Raise your hand and repeat after me."

Mac did as he was told.

"I, Luke MacKenzie, promise to treat my library books with care, read them promptly and return them before the due date, so help me God."

Chuckling, Mac repeated the promise and when he was finished, she handed him the paper. "Thanks," he said.

"Is there anything I can help you find? What do you like to read? Besides Shakespeare."

"I've been reading the biographies of the great explorers—Columbus, Marco Polo, Amundsen."

"That sounds interesting."

"What do you like to read?"

She took a moment to formulate an answer. "My favorite is true-life adventure. Climbing Everest and surviving in a life raft for seventy days. Books about people with daring and courage."

"And do you have daring and courage?" he asked.

"No," Emma said. "Quite the opposite. That's why I find those books so fascinating."

"Note to self," he murmured. "Add more adventure to Marry-Me Emma's life."

She giggled softly and her cheeks turned a pretty shade of pink. "There's a new biography of David Livingstone. If you haven't read it, you should. I thought it was excellent."

"Good. I'll read it. And maybe we could get together and have coffee and talk about it."

"Are you asking me on a date?"

Mac had never needed to clarify his intent when it came to women, but he wasn't quite sure if coffee and a book discussion qualified as a date. "Would you consider that a date?" he asked.

Emma thought about her answer for a long moment. "Probably not."

"What would I have to add to make it a real date?" Mac asked.

"Maybe dinner? Definitely dinner. And a movie? But we don't have a theater in town, so dinner would be enough."

She blushed more deeply and Mac could see that the question had flustered her. "Emma, would you like to go out to dinner with me?"

She drew in a sharp breath, then nodded her head. "Yes. Yes, that would be lovely. When?"

"Soon? But I'm probably going to need three or four days to finish the book."

"Or I could recommend a shorter book," she said.

"How about Saturday?"

"The Livingstone bio is about four hundred and fifty pages long, including the notes and index."

"I'm a fast reader," Mac assured her.

"It's a date, then. Saturday night."

Mac wanted to stay longer, to find an excuse to grab her hand or steal a kiss. But he had officially secured a date with Emma and, considering her unpredictable nature, he thought it best to leave while he was ahead.

"I'm going to go now, before I find a way to screw this up. I'll see you Saturday night."

"Where?" she asked.

"Great question. Any thoughts?"

"I'll pick you up at the hangar and we'll decide then."

She smiled and Mac felt his blood warm a few degrees. "Good idea."

"Enjoy the book, Mac," she murmured.

"See you Saturday, Emma," he said.

As he walked back upstairs to the circulation desk, Mac smiled to himself. He'd managed to play that perfectly, yet he hadn't a clue how it had all happened. When he'd set out to find her, he hadn't been sure she'd agree to a date.

With the exception of their love of books, they had absolutely nothing in common. She was a homebody, content in a small town, living a small life. Her only adventures came from books. She'd put down roots and was a respected member of the community. Emma had history that included friends and family.

Mac had no roots, no family, no past. He'd spent his adult life drifting from place to place, taking work when he needed it. Everything he owned fit into his plane. His freedom was all he'd ever required in life. He had nothing to offer a woman like Emma.

So why was he so determined to charm her, Mac wondered. Did he see her as a challenge? Or did he want to experience just a tiny bit of the life he'd never had? Or was she just so amazing that he couldn't help himself?

"It's just a date. You're not climbing Everest."

It *was* only dinner, and yet somehow Mac felt that it was the start of so much more.

2

The normally quiet library came alive after school when students strolled through the front door and took their customary spots at the reading tables. The students who wanted to study usually chose to stay at the school library. But Emma had a loyal group of outsiders, kids who either weren't comfortable at school or had been kicked out of the school library for bad behavior. The former she welcomed, the latter, she considered a challenge to be won over.

"Where are the books about T. rex?"

Emma smiled at Joey Hammersmith. "See that big green dino over there? Right underneath him."

"Thanks!"

Joey ran off and her gaze fell on a young girl who'd been part of the after-school crowd for the past few months. She appeared to be about eleven or twelve and always sat at the same table, in the same chair. Emma caught her eye and smiled, but the girl quickly looked back down at her books.

"What time is your date tomorrow night?"

Trisha leaned over the counter and pulled out the lollipop container, grabbing a root beer-flavored sucker for herself. She held out the container to Emma. "Join me?"

"I'm on a diet," Emma said. "I bought a new dress for the date and I—"

"Oh, is it a dress kind of date?" Trisha inquired. "I just assumed it would be a jeans date."

Emma frowned. "Why would you think that?"

"I don't know. Just from the way you described him. He seemed more like a casual kind of guy."

"He didn't really specify," Emma said. "Crap, now I'm going to have to go buy a new pair of jeans. And stop eating completely for the next twenty-four hours."

"Why don't you just call him and ask?"

The idea of phoning him caused a flood of nerves. There was something about Luke MacKenzie that turned her into a stammering schoolgirl. And now that she'd decided he was going to be "the one," she couldn't think about him without picturing the guy naked and lying in her bed.

"Maybe I should just go with a casual skirt and sweater," Emma decided. "It will be appropriate for either kind of date. And I won't have to diet at all." She grabbed the lollipop container and fished out a raspberry pop. "Did you stop by just to make me nervous?"

"Of course not," Trisha said. She studied her shrewdly. "So do you think you're going to do it tonight?"

Emma groaned. "I don't believe he's a sleep-with-a-woman-on-the-first-date kind of guy. He seems very passionate, but he might also be a closet gentleman."

"Just be careful, Em."

"I bought condoms."

"That's not the kind of careful I was talking about. This is a small town full of gossips, and you know how people feel about you. If you start romping about with some stranger, people are going to talk. Especially those ladies on the library board."

"Don't worry about me. Besides, it's not as if we're going to have a relationship or anything," Emma said. "Can I do anything for you?"

"I need Keats. Every book of his poetry that you have on the shelf."

"You know where that section is," she said. Trisha was about to leave when Emma called her name and motioned her closer. "See that girl over there? With the blond hair and the red sweater?"

Trisha glanced in the direction of Emma's gaze and nodded. "Lily. Lily Harper. She's a foster child with Dave and Denise Prentiss. I've heard they're planning to adopt her."

"She's here every day after school. And she always sits alone. Doesn't she have any friends?"

Trisha shook her head. "I don't think so. She's bounced around a lot from what I've heard."

"What happened to her parents?"

"I'm not sure. She's not from around here, and she doesn't talk about herself."

"She seems so sad. And she never checks anything out. She pulls books from the shelves and reads them here, but never takes anything home."

Emma felt a sort of kinship with the little girl. She understood how it felt to be an outsider. After the brace and the acne, her friends had started to distance themselves from her and she'd been alone. Books had become her best friends and she'd lived through the characters she loved. They had wonderful friends who shared amazing adventures.

"Are we still going to the flea market tomorrow?" Trisha asked.

"Why wouldn't we?"

"I thought you might want the time at home before your big date."

"I'd just spend the time obsessing over it. I need distractions."

"Then I'll pick you up at nine," she said. "But right now I have to go find my books and then I'm going to pick up a very large pizza for dinner. When are you done with work? Do you want to join us?"

"I close tonight. But let's stop for breakfast on the way to the flea market. At that pancake place."

"So much for the diet."

"I'm wearing a skirt, remember. I think I'll be safe."

While Trisha went upstairs to find her books, Emma walked over to the young adult section and found one of her favorite books. She slowly approached Lily, then slid the book across the table. "Have you read this series?" she asked.

Lily stared at the book, then shook her head. "I-Is it good?"

She risked a look up and Emma nodded. "It was one of my favorites when I was your age. And you can take it home to read. I can get you a library card."

The girl shook her head. "I'll read it here," she murmured.

"All right. But I'd still like to give you a library card. It's free. Then, if you decide you want to take something home you can."

Lily shrugged. "Okay. Thanks."

"I'll have it waiting at the desk. You can pick it up before you leave."

"Do you know my name?"

"It's Lily Harper. You live with the Prentiss family."

Lily nodded again, her gaze falling to the book that Emma had offered her. "Yeah," she murmured. "1810 Birch Street."

"If you'd like me to find more books for you, just tell me what you enjoy reading and I can make some suggestions."

"Okay," she said.

"I'm usually here after school. But if I'm not, you can leave me a note."

She was filling out the forms for Lily's library card when a bouquet of flowers appeared in front of her computer screen. Emma turned to find Mac grinning at her. "Hello," she said.

"Hi."

Emma took the bouquet. "What are you doing here?"

"I just thought I'd stop in and firm up our plans for tomorrow night. Get some suggestions on where you might want to go for dinner. And see if you have any opinions on *Oklahoma*."

"Oklahoma? I've never been there, but I suppose it's a nice place to live if you like…farming?"

"No, *Oklahoma* the musical. The local community theater is doing the play and I thought I'd get us tickets."

Emma giggled. "You enjoy musical theater?"

"Well, there's no movie theater in town, so this would be the next best choice. It could be really good."

"It could also be really bad," Emma said.

"I bet it will be fun, you'll see."

She wasn't sure "fun" was what she wanted for their date. She wanted something romantic, something that would put them both in the mood for seduction. She was hoping the night would end in a tangle of sheets and sweaty bodies and she wasn't sure that an amateur production of *Oklahoma* would lead them there.

"Buddy's mechanic, J.J., has got a pretty big role," Mac added. "He's got a decent singing voice."

"He used to be in all the shows in high school," Emma said.

"Right. I forgot you knew each other."

"Everyone knows everyone else in this town. If you have any deep, dark secrets, you better spill them now because sooner or later, they'll be found out."

Mac braced his elbows on the counter and leaned closer. "There is one thing," he murmured, his eyes dark, his voice mysterious. "But I can't really tell you here. Is there somewhere we could go? Someplace more private?"

Emma held her breath. What kind of secret was he about to reveal? Was he running from the law? Was he married? Had he nefarious motives for asking her out? "My office," she said breathlessly.

He followed behind her to the door near the end of the circulation desk. The moment the door closed behind them, Mac wrapped his arm around her waist and pulled her body against his. His lips came down on hers and, before she could protest, Emma was caught in a deep and passionate kiss.

His hands skimmed along her rib cage and then, just a moment later, were tangled in her hair. Emma's knees went weak and she stumbled, bracing herself against a bookcase. When he finally drew back, she took a ragged breath and tried to regain her composure. "What was that?" she murmured.

"If you don't know, then I wasn't doing it right."

She laughed softly. "Oh, no, you did it right."

"Good. Because I've been thinking about kissing you since the last time we were together. And thinking isn't as nice as actually doing it."

A shiver skittered through her body and she nodded, knowing his words were truer that even he realized. "I—I should get back out there. If you leave the kids alone for too long they'll find some way to get into trouble."

"All right," he said, twisting his fingers through hers. He pulled her hand up to his lips and pressed a kiss below her wrist. "I'll see you tomorrow night. Oh, and I'll pick you up at your place. Buddy lets me use his truck and I got it all cleaned up."

"Do you know where I live?"

"I'll ask around," Mac said. "I'm sure someone will be happy to tell me."

They walked out of the office and he waved as he walked toward the front entrance. Emma took another shaky breath. Oh, they'd tell him. But what else would they say? she wondered. Would he find out she was a virgin? And if he did, was he hoping to change her sexual status in the near future?

Emma groaned inwardly. This was exactly what she'd been waiting for all these years. Now was not the time to chicken out. If she expected to lure him into bed, she'd need to be confident, or he'd never believe she was a willing partner.

She closed her eyes and cursed beneath her breath. This was like any fear of the unknown. When it was over, it would seem easy in retrospect. She'd laugh at her fears, just as the adventurers in her books did.

"Do you have my card?"

Emma dragged her eyes away from the computer screen and found Lily Harper waiting, her backpack strap slung over one shoulder. "Do you have any books you'd like to take home?"

The girl shook her head, then placed the young adult novel that Emma had given her onto the counter. "Thank you."

"You don't want to take this home?"

"I'll read it here," she said.

"Is there anything else I can help you with?"

She opened her mouth, then quickly snapped it shut. Emma held out the library card and Lily snatched it from her fingers and hurried out of the library. Emma drew a deep breath and sighed. Childhood was such a complicated time for some kids. She couldn't help but empathize with Lily Harper, so scared and vulnerable. At times like this, Emma wished she had more than books to offer.

She picked up the bouquet that Mac had brought her and drew in the scent of the flowers. All the troubles of her own adolescence had made her into the woman she was today. But her lack of sexual experience kept her anchored to that vulnerable girl. She couldn't truly feel like an adult until she'd left that part of her behind. And she was determined that Mac would be the one to help her do that.

MAC SORTED THROUGH the stack of scribbled notes, then stared at the computer screen. He was supposed to enter his crop-dusting jobs into the accounting program so invoices could be generated, but Buddy's program was ancient and nothing seemed to work properly.

The screen door creaked and he looked up to see Charlie Clemmons standing in the late morning sun, a large plastic bag tucked under his arm. Mac straightened, shoving the bookkeeping aside. "Hi," he said. "What can I do for you?"

Charlie approached the counter, reaching to pull his wallet from the back pocket of his jeans. He cleared his throat nervously. "I want to hire you again to fly another banner for me."

Mac shook his head, holding out his hands. "Listen, Charlie, I get how you feel—"

"This is different," Charlie insisted. "I bought a new banner. I want you to take it up this morning. She and Trisha always meet for coffee on Saturdays so she'll be sure to see it."

"Emma Bryant came in here after the last banner," Mac said. "She was pretty angry. I don't think a new banner is going to make her happy."

"This one will make her very happy," Charlie said. "I've decided that I was moving too fast. I have to slow down and court her. A girl like Emma doesn't want a pushy guy. A girl like Emma needs time to fall in love."

"A girl like Emma?" Mac asked.

Charlie shifted uneasily. "Yeah…you know."

"I do?"

"Yeah. 'Cause she's a virgin." He paused. "Not that there's anything wrong with that. In fact, to be honest, I'm lacking in that department, too. That's why we'd be an excellent match. There wouldn't be any…expectations."

Mac groaned inwardly. This was too much information! Was this the gossip that Emma had referred to? Mac let the information sink in. Though it didn't change his desire for her, it certainly changed his attitude about seducing her at the next available opportunity. One didn't just ravish a virgin without a care for her limited experience. Being a woman's first lover was a tremendous responsibility—the kind of responsibility he wasn't sure he was ready to accept.

"So what will it take?" Charlie asked.

Mac blinked and met his gaze. "What?"

"What will it take to get you to fly my banner? I paid you two hundred dollars for the last flight. I assume this one will cost the same?"

"Are you sure you want to waste—I mean, spend—your money on this? I've talked to Emma and she really isn't impressed. Maybe you ought to turn your attention to another woman. Someone more…obliging."

"What does that mean?"

"A girl who might welcome your affections?"

"But the book said that I should be persistent and not give up. No matter what." Charlie pulled a dog-earred paperback out of his jacket pocket and dropped it on the counter.

"How to Catch a Mate in Ten Easy Lessons," Mac read out loud. "Which lesson are you on?"

"I can't seem to get past number three," Charlie said with a dejected sigh.

"Maybe you should start over…with a different woman. A guy has to know when to cut his losses and move on." Mac couldn't help but feel a little guilty for his suggestion. After all, he did have ulterior motives. But it wasn't just because he'd been suddenly captivated by Emma Bryant and wanted her for himself. He also wanted to save her the irritation and embarrassment of dealing with another of Charlie's banners.

Charlie set the banner on the counter. "You're probably right. You might as well toss that," he said.

Mac nodded. "Good call. You'll see. You'll find someone who'll appreciate your romantic gestures. There are a lot of fish in the sea."

"Where? What sea have you been looking in? There are only so many women in this town who'd consider dating a guy like me and I've run through them all."

"Maybe you ought to aim higher," Mac suggested. "Shoot for a girl who's out of your league."

"The book doesn't help with that," Charlie said. "I wouldn't know what to do."

Mac paused. If he really wanted a clear road ahead with Emma, then he had to be willing to help Charlie out. It wasn't as if business was booming for Buddy's Flying Services. And he did have knowledge he could impart. "How about if I help you out?" Mac offered.

"You'd do that?" Charlie asked. "Why?"

"Because I don't want to see you make a fool out

of yourself. We'll hang out. The 49ers are playing on Monday night. Is there a sports bar around here?"

"There's Shooters just east of town."

"All right. I'll meet you there on Monday night. We'll have a few beers, talk to a few women and see where it goes."

"You'll be my wingman," Charlie said, grinning. "That's been my problem all along. No wingman."

Charlie left the banner sitting on the counter. It was still there when J.J. came in through the shop door. He stopped and stared at it, then winced, shaking his head. "Charlie again?"

"I talked him out of it," Mac explained.

J.J. seemed surprised. "That guy is like a terrier with a bone. He once decided that he was going to get on that show *Gladiator Games*. He trained for three years. By the time he was ready, the show had been canceled. Charlie has the worst luck. That's why people avoid him. They're afraid it might rub off on them."

"I'm just going to distract the guy for a while. Give him some good advice and maybe find him a different girl."

J.J. gave Mac a dubious look. "You're fixin' to steal his girl away."

"Emma is not *his girl*."

"That's not what most people in town believe. Most folks around here are all for the match."

"You didn't mention that she was a virgin," Mac said.

J.J. shook his head. "Why should that make a difference to you?"

"It doesn't," Mac said. "It's just something most

guys would want to know." He cursed beneath his breath. This was suddenly getting far too complicated. Too many people had a stake in his relationship with Emma. Mac had always preferred to keep his social and sexual life simple. It made for easier exits. And he'd be the first person to admit that he never wanted to stick around for long.

He was all too familiar with the consequences. There would be questions—about his parents, his family, his background. Where was he born? What were his parents' names? What about grandparents? So many questions that he didn't have answers for.

For any other man, that might have made a difference. But for Luke MacKenzie—or whatever his name really was—he'd put those questions aside. He'd determined at a young age to let the past go, to focus purely on the present.

Hell, it made for a much happier life. The past was all about mistakes and regrets, lost opportunities and broken promises. And the future? Well, that was about goals and dreams and aspirations. All those things just out of a guy's reach.

It was, and always would be about the present for Mac. He knew all too well that life could change in a split second. Dreams could be shattered and the future turned upside down. His mind flashed an image of that night, of the empty motel room and the police cars outside. So many questions and never any answers.

So he lived for pleasure and adventure, excitement and spontaneity. He never knew what the new day would bring, but Mac was always determined to make the best of it.

"Any idea how to work this computer?" Mac asked, turning to J.J.

"Yeah," the mechanic said. "What's the problem?"

"I have to enter these time slips and fuel receipts to generate an invoice and I can't figure out what I'm doing wrong."

J.J. grabbed the stack of notes. "It would take me longer to explain than it would to do the invoices," he said. "I can take care of it."

"Are you sure?"

"No problem," J.J. said.

"Can you keep an eye on the front desk? I have something I need to do."

"I have to leave in an hour. We have some final work on the set before the show tonight. You still planning on coming?"

"Yeah, absolutely," Mac said. "Wouldn't miss it for the world."

"I wouldn't go that far," J.J. joked. "I'm not that good."

Mac chuckled and clapped J.J. on the back. "Don't sell yourself short."

Mac walked out into the hangar and pulled open the passenger door of his plane. It was the closest thing he had to a home. Mac crawled through to the tail, rummaging around until he found what he was looking for. He took the small tin box out and sat down on a crate, pulling off the lid in the light of day.

The rusty tin held all that was left of his old life—his only clues to his past. He picked up the larger of the two wedding bands and stared down at it, then slipped it on his finger. Marriage had never been a part of his future. Until he had a past, he couldn't have a future. But how did one go about finding ghosts? The police had tried and failed.

Did he even want to find them? Wouldn't it simply be easier to know nothing? And why did it make a difference now?

Mac closed his eyes. Emma. For some reason, she made him think about the future, made him question his past.

But why? He'd met her only a few days ago. There had to be a reason for this unreasonable attraction. Some quality that had captured his attention. It wasn't her virginity. Had he been aware of that, he would have run in the opposite direction. Charlie was right—there were too many expectations.

And yet, the news hadn't changed his interest in her. Emma was smart and beautiful and vulnerable and strong. She was the kind of woman who needed a partner to help her navigate the world, yet would never admit she couldn't do everything alone. But was he that man?

Mac slipped the wedding ring off his finger and held it up to the light. His gaze focused on the inside of the ring. "For Benjamin, with love," he read.

Who the hell was Benjamin and what was Mac doing with his wedding ring?

Mac tossed the ring back into the box. Probing the past was too dangerous. He'd been right before. It was better to live in the present.

"I'M READY," EMMA SAID, holding the phone to her ear. "I've been going over it in my head all day long and I'm ready."

"This is a dinner date," Trish said, her voice crackling over the connection. "Not the D-Day Invasion."

"I realize that. But I have to have a plan, don't you think? We'll have dinner, we'll discuss the book, have a little wine and then, sometime around dessert, I'll make my proposition."

"I thought you guys were going to see *Oklahoma*."

"I hope that's just his backup plan, in case the date is a real disaster."

"Maybe you shouldn't plan too much. Just let it happen," Trish said. "You know, organically."

"And here I was thinking I'd just force the issue up front and forget about the date entirely." Emma stood in front of the mirror and studied her reflection critically. "Why is this so complicated?"

"It isn't. Thousands of couples go out on first dates. And hundreds of them go home afterward and have wild monkey sex without suffering even the tiniest twinge of guilt. You bought condoms, didn't you?"

"Four different kinds," Emma said. "I had to drive all the way into Petaluma to get them. You should have seen the look I got from the clerk. I think she assumed I was going to an orgy." Emma groaned. "I have to go. I hear his car. Wish me luck."

"You don't need luck," Trish said. "Just be yourself and see where it goes. No pressure, no expectations."

Emma switched off her phone, then checked her appearance once more. She looked nice. She'd taken extra time with her hair and put on a tiny bit of mascara and lipstick. The outfit she wore wasn't blatantly sexy, but it hugged her body in all the right places.

A knock sounded from the front door and Emma

jumped, pressing her hand to her heart. Her pulse began to race as she approached the door, and for a moment, she felt light-headed and dizzy. She drew a few deep breaths, then pasted a smile on her face. Emma reached for the door handle and swung it open. Mac stood outside, another bouquet of flowers clutched in his hand.

"Hi, there," he said with a wide grin. "You look great."

"Thank you," she murmured. "So do you."

Emma's hand trembled as she reached for the flowers. His hand brushed against hers. The touch was enough to send a shock wave coursing through her body and when he grabbed hold of her fingers, her pulse leaped.

For a long moment they stood frozen, neither one of them ready to move. But then, Emma groaned softly and threw herself into his arms. They stumbled inside the house, her lips searching for his before settling in to a deeply passionate kiss.

This wasn't the way things were supposed to begin. But as his tongue tasted the warm depths of her mouth, she forgot all about her plans and decided to surrender herself to fate.

His hands spanned her waist as Mac pressed her against the wall, his hips meeting hers. The control had suddenly shifted. Emma had never been kissed like this, with such single-minded desire and such overwhelming passion. It was as if he'd lost the capacity to think and was operating only on sexual instinct.

Her heart pounded out a quick rhythm. She tried to catch her breath and when she couldn't, she stepped back, gasping, her face flushed with warmth. "Sorry," she said in a shaky tone.

Mac pressed his forehead against hers. "Is everything all right?"

Emma shook her head. She felt as if she was about to pass out. "No, it's not. I don't think I can do this."

"Kiss me?"

"All of it," she said, throwing her arms into the air. She walked across the room, putting a safe distance between them. "I thought it would be easy. But it's always just looming on the horizon, this huge, black cloud that at any moment is going to surround me and smother me with guilt and shame and—"

"What are you talking about?" Mac asked.

Emma began laughing and suddenly she couldn't stop. Why was this so difficult? Women lost their virginities every day. And yet the longer she held on to hers, the more it seemed to define her.

"Are you all right?"

It was one of those laughing fits that left her gasping and crying at the same time. She grabbed a quick breath. "It's just—you're going to hear this anyway if you haven't already and maybe it best that I just said it up front."

"Say what? That you're a virgin?"

"I'm a virgin," Emma shouted, throwing her arms out. She snapped her mouth shut and stared at him. "You knew?" She pressed her fingertips to her lips and waited for the humiliation to pass. She hadn't meant to just blurt it out, but it was like an embarrassing medical condition. There was just no way to work it into the conversation.

"Yeah, I heard something about it," he said.

Emma took a ragged breath. "I wanted you to understand. I mean, it's best to be honest and I—"

"And you assumed I'd expect the evening to end in bed?"

"I was hoping it would," she said. "At least that's how I wanted to feel. But then, that kiss just—wow! I mean, my life flashed before my eyes and I couldn't think. Or maybe I couldn't stop thinking. I don't know. I'm so confused."

He frowned, then shook his head. "I don't understand."

She turned away from him and began to pace, following a short track across the living room. "I want to be completely up front with you. I don't really care about dinner or talking about the book or going to see the play. I was just really hoping that you'd find me attractive enough to seduce at the end of the evening."

"I do find you very attractive," he murmured, reaching out to grab her hand. He pulled her back toward him, then rested his hands on her hips. "And seducing you has been on my mind a lot."

"Before or after you found out I was a virgin?" He paused before answering and she could see the truth in his eyes. "I get it. It's a big deal. Huge."

"It's just that your first time is supposed to be special," Mac explained. "Especially if you've waited this long for it to happen."

"And you can't make it special?"

"Sure I could. But you'll want more than a quick fix."

"No, no, no," Emma said, shaking her head. "I don't

want a boyfriend or a fiancé. I just want sex." She slapped her hand over her mouth. "Maybe we should call an end to this now, before I make a complete fool of myself."

He took her hand and pulled her over to the sofa, tugging her down to sit beside him. "What do you want to do, Emma? Right now."

"I want to crawl under a rock and stay there until you forget this whole conversation," she said.

"That's not necessary. Let's put aside all the talk about the…the deflowering."

Emma groaned and covered her face with her hands. "Oh, don't call it that. I don't have flowers down there that need to be picked."

"What am I supposed to call it?"

"I don't know. Call it…call it, the task at hand."

"Are you interested in someone who will simply complete *the task at hand*, or do you want more?"

"Just the task," she said. "Nothing more."

"No romance, no dating, no dinner and a movie?"

Emma shook her head. "Just the task."

"You're sure?"

She nodded.

"You've given me a lot to consider. I guess I'll let you know."

"You have to consider it? I thought men were able to just do it." She drew a ragged breath. "Is it because you don't find me attractive?"

Didn't all single men love sex? And she'd assumed they weren't very discriminating about where they got it. Was her offer that repulsive to him?

He chuckled. "No. I find you incredibly attractive, as I mentioned at the beginning."

"Then why don't you want to—do the task?"

He paused, as if to collect his thoughts. "Emma, you're the kind of woman who deserves the best in life. You deserve so much more than I can give you."

"You can't give me a single night of mind-blowing sex? Because that's really all I want. Just one night."

"One night," Mac murmured. "All right, I'll get back to you. I promise."

With that, he turned on his heel and walked to the front door. But Emma couldn't leave it at that. She ran after him and grabbed his arm. "You think I'm crazy, don't you? That's it."

He shook his head. "No, I think you've taken a very sensible approach to your problem."

"Exactly. It's sensible. I'm Emma, the virgin librarian. You're Mac, the handsome, itinerant pilot. It makes perfect sense."

"Does it? I mean, what are you going to do after it's finished? It's kind of a life-changing event." He met her gaze.

"That's just it. I want it to change my life. So it *isn't* my life."

"May I ask you something?"

Emma nodded. "Yes, of course. Ask me anything."

"We've established that you're twenty-seven years old and you're still a virgin. We've also established that you're beautiful and smart and sexy. Just how is that possible? Is this some sort of religious thing?"

"No. It just happened. I've never dated much, never had serious boyfriends. Believe it or not, the opportunity only presented itself a few times when I was younger and I decided to turn it down. And then the years just got away from me."

"And you want me to take care of this for you?"

"Yes, I would appreciate that. It would only be one night. Not even a full night. I mean, it could go pretty fast, I think. At least that's what I've heard. And I can guarantee that it wouldn't be horrible. I've done a lot of reading so I know what's what."

"You realize that being aware that this is your first time changes everything."

"I'm kind of just getting that," Emma said. "Why, though? It's still sex."

"There's a lot of pressure," Mac said.

"You mean performance anxiety? Believe me, I can relate. Is that why you're afraid to…do the deed?"

Mac cursed beneath his breath. "No. I don't get performance anxiety."

"Then why?"

He thought about her question for a long moment, then shrugged. "Maybe *I* want more," he murmured. "Maybe a one-night stand isn't enough for me."

The notion that a man like Mac might prefer romance over pure lust surprised her. On the surface, he seemed to be the perfect playboy type, a guy who could easily love 'em, then leave 'em.

"I don't expect it to be special," Emma said.

"I want to make it special for you," Mac said. He glanced over at her and smiled. "Listen, why don't we just delay negotiations on this tonight and pick it up at a later date."

"I understand," Emma said. "If you don't want to, you can just say so. I won't be hurt."

"Oh, I want to," he replied. "Believe me, I've been thinking about it since the moment you walked into the shop. But I'm not sure you understand what you're asking. So I'd like to take a little time."

"All right. But if you change your mind, just call."

"I will," Mac assured her. "There is one thing we could do right now."

"What's that?" Emma asked. It all happened so quickly, she didn't have a chance to prepare. He slipped his arm around her waist and pulled her close, his gaze meeting hers. And in a heartbeat, his mouth came down on hers in a long, delicious kiss.

Emma had already grown to love the way he kissed. His attention fixed on her lips for just a moment before his mouth descended on hers. And after that, a wild whirl of sensations assailed her body. His kiss was a demand, not a request, and she had no choice but to respond.

When he finally drew away, his eyes were closed and her breath came in short gasps. A thrill raced through her. It was obvious the kiss had affected him in the same way it had her. Maybe she should count this as a victory.

"I'll talk to you soon?" she asked.

"You will," he said.

She walked him to the front door and opened it. "Thanks for the kiss. It was really nice."

"Emma?"

"Yes?"

"You don't ever have to thank me for kissing you."

3

MAC CIRCLED BUDDY'S PLANE, checking all the fittings and controls for crop dusting. He was due to go out at dawn the next morning, and he wanted to get a jump on the job. Hell, he didn't have anything better to do on a Sunday than catch up with work at the shop.

He wasn't going to fly his own plane because Mac's old deHaviland Beaver wasn't typically used for agriculture applications like crop dusting, a job better suited to a small, maneuverable plane. The Beaver was made for transport—of people and their belongings.

Whether he was bush piloting in Alaska or transporting produce in the warmer climates of California, Mac's plane was the closest thing he had to a home. When he had no place to live, he slept in the tail section.

J.J. watched him as he went through his check, sipping on a cold Yoo-hoo. "So, how did your date go? I didn't see you at the show last night."

"It didn't go. We decided to postpone the date." He glanced over his shoulder. "Sorry about the show."

"What happened?"

"It's far too complicated to explain. We were looking for different things, I guess."

"You were looking for sex, she was looking for romance?"

Mac shook his head. "No. The exact opposite. She was hoping for an end to her 'condition' and I wasn't willing to provide it. At least not under her terms."

"Terms?"

Mac ran his hand through his hair. "I don't know. Maybe I should have said yes. But there's something about Emma that I can't get my mind around. I don't want her to view me as just some solution to a problem."

It didn't make sense. He ought to be thrilled that she was interested in no-strings sex. And there was no doubt in his mind that their intimacy would be more than just one night. Once she got a taste of what he could offer in the bedroom, she'd want more.

So why did he refuse? Why not take the chance that he could turn a single night of sex into something more?

But it wouldn't ultimately be his choice. In this case, Emma was entirely in control. And Mac didn't relish the thought of being discarded. Too many bad memories had been attached to that particular feeling.

"I've never met anyone like her," Mac said. He cursed softly, shaking his head. "She is…complicated. A puzzle I'm determined to solve."

"That's probably why she isn't married," J.J. said. "Didn't she date in high school?"

"Not much. She had to wear this brace on her back

and kids made fun of her. She just kept out of the way. She was really shy and kind of a mess. Braces, acne. And then, after high school, her mother got sick and she had to care for her. I guess she didn't have time for dates."

"But she's beautiful and sexy. And smart." He stepped away from the plane. "I think the real reason runs a lot deeper. There's something else going on with her." He sighed. He'd wasted too much energy already trying to make sense of Emma Bryant. "Let's get out of here. There has to be some football game on somewhere. Why don't we go grab ourselves a few beers and relax."

"I'm supposed to help out at the firehouse at two. They have their big chicken barbecue today. You should come. Emma will be there."

"How do you know?"

"She's there every year. They have a cake walk and she always makes her mom's favorite cake. It goes for big money. Charlie's won it the last three years."

"Charlie will be there, too?"

"Everyone in town goes. It's a big deal. Come on. It'll be fun. And they have beer there."

Though J.J. wanted to leave right away, Mac insisted that he take the time for a quick shower and shave. He found a pair of clean jeans and a chambray shirt, then slipped into a well-worn canvas jacket.

When he got into J.J.'s truck, the mechanic wrinkled his nose. "Went a little overboard on the cologne there, Sparky?"

"Is it too much?" He reached for the door. "I'll go wash it off."

"Nah, don't bother. I'm just used to the smell of oil and aviation fuel." J.J. shook his head. "Besides, the entire fire station smells like barbecued chicken. You'll be fine."

They arrived at the fire station about ten minutes later, parking J.J.'s truck a few blocks away and walking toward the music coming from a live bluegrass band.

Mac had lived in a lot of different places over the years—large cities, small towns, even a few places in the wilderness of Alaska and Wyoming. He couldn't recall feeling more at home than he did in San Coronado. Though he'd been around for only a few weeks, people seemed to know him on sight and always had a friendly greeting.

The town was practically one giant family, and for someone like Emma, he could understand how that could be both a blessing and a curse. She didn't have any relatives close by, so her friends in town were always there to back her up. Yet, they also seemed to have some pretty strong opinions on how she should live her life.

"Before we go inside, let me give you one piece of advice," J.J. said.

"Shoot."

"Be careful. As quickly as these folks can be your friend, they can also turn against you. If they think your intentions with Emma are anything less than honorable, they'll make living here nearly impossible—for you, and for her."

"They're that bad?"

"There was a computer salesman who was courting

her a few years back. He made a few remarks in a bar one night that didn't go over well. They ran him out of town the next morning and he hasn't been seen since. As far as these folks are concerned, Charlie's the top dog until Emma officially rejects him."

"I thought she had."

"Not publicly. She probably doesn't want to embarrass him. But until she does say something, or he moves on, just be careful."

Mac nodded. He'd never really had to deal with these kinds of problems, he mused. In the past, when he wanted a woman, he just turned on the charm and went after her, full speed ahead. But if he wasn't careful, he'd be forced to leave the first place he'd felt comfortable in years, not to mention possibly hurt Emma in the process.

The moment they stepped inside the huge garage, Mac scanned the crowd for Emma. He saw her standing with another woman near a table full of fancy cakes. "I'll see you later," he said to J.J.

But as he wove through the crowd toward her, he noticed Charlie doing the same from the opposite direction. They met in front of Emma and she glanced back and forth between them, a bemused smile curling the corners of her mouth. "Hi, Charlie. Hi, Mac."

"Hi," they both said in tandem.

"Do you know him?" Charlie asked, nodding at Mac.

"I do," Emma said. "I lodged a complaint with him about those banners you keep flying."

"We know each other," Mac said. "We're…friends."

"More like acquaintances," Emma corrected, sending him a coy smile.

"No, I'd say good friends," Mac countered. "Maybe a little more than good friends. Close friends. We haven't been acquainted long, but we're…close."

Charlie looked back and forth between the two of them, a suspicious glint in his eye. "So this is why you were trying to warn me off?" he said, his gaze fixed on Mac. "You are officially fired as my wingman."

"This is my friend, Trisha," she said. "Trisha, this is Mac."

He said hello to Trisha and she returned the greeting.

"What does he mean? You tried to warn him off?" Emma asked.

Mac shrugged. "He brought another banner in on Saturday. I told him you wouldn't be happy if I took it up. I'm right, aren't I?"

"He's right," Emma said to Charlie. "You have to stop this. I'm not in love with you. I'm sorry, but I'm not."

"You just need some time," Charlie said.

"No, I don't—"

At that moment the public address system crackled. "Ladies and gents, it's time for the cake auction. Get out your wallets and bid on some of the best-tasting cakes in all of California. First up is the offering by our lovely librarian, Emma Bryant. She brings us her mama's favorite recipe for Lady Baltimore Cake. So step on up here and let's sell this sweet treat."

"I'm going to win that cake," Charlie said.

"I wouldn't be so sure about that," Mac countered.

"Don't," Emma said, grabbing Mac's arm. "They get ridiculous amounts for these auction items. I'll make you one for free."

"What fun would that be?" Mac asked. "Besides, this might finally snuff out that giant torch that Charlie Clemmons carries around for you."

"You know how stubborn he is. He'll pay three thousand dollars if he has to. Do you have that kind of money?"

Mac grinned. Living like a bum had given him plenty of opportunities to put aside a few dollars now and then. "I have half a million sitting in a bank in San Francisco. You think it will go for that much?"

Emma gasped, her eyes going wide. "Don't you dare bid any more than two thousand. Promise me you won't."

The moment the auction started, the crowd grew quiet. It was as if everyone present knew what was going on. Miss Bryant, town librarian, had two gentleman suitors and they were about to declare themselves for her.

The bidding started small, moving up in ten-dollar increments. But when they reached two hundred dollars, Mac suddenly jumped the bid by fifty dollars. A cheer went up from the crowd and he grinned.

"I can't watch this," Emma muttered.

"It's like an old-fashioned duel," Trisha said. "Only with cake!"

By the time the price got above one thousand, the bidding increments had grown to one hundred dollars. It was clear that Charlie was determined to win and that Mac felt the same way.

When the price reached two thousand, Emma had clearly had enough. She pushed her way through the crowd. "Stop!" she shouted. "That's enough."

"We're not done," Charlie growled.

"I'll make another cake," she said. "If you both stop bidding now, you'll both get one. The same cake, I promise. Just give the man his money and I'll take care of all the details."

The crowd roared their approval and Emma turned to Charlie. "Please?"

"All right," Charlie said.

Mac nodded and the auctioneer banged his gavel. Before either of the boys could grab the cake, Emma snatched it up herself. "Now, I'm taking my cake and going home."

"Emma, don't," Trisha cried.

"I'll take you home," Charlie said.

"No, I will," Mac said.

"I'll walk. I only live a few blocks away. And I don't want either one of you following me."

THE AUCTION FOR the next cake had already begun, shifting the attention of the crowd. Emma made her way through the crowd to the door, a tight smile on her face, the cake box tucked beneath her arm.

Her humiliation was complete. The entire town had seen what had happened between Charlie and Mac, and all over a silly cake. As she started down the street, she heard footsteps behind her and she spun around. "Stop following me!"

"Em, hold up. I'll walk you home."

"Go away, Mac. I don't want to talk to you."

As she continued her escape, the wind picked up and Emma could smell rain in the air. She increased her pace and was nearly home when the skies opened up and a cold rain began to pour down in sheets, soaking her to the skin. Emma stood on the porch and searched for her keys. Glancing over her shoulder, she spotted him watching her from the sidewalk. "Go away, Mac. Leave me alone." She fumbled with the lock, trying to balance the soggy cake box beneath her arm.

A moment later, his warm hands covered hers. "Let me," he murmured.

Reluctantly, she handed him the key and stepped back. When the door was open, she stepped inside, then turned to him. "You can't come in."

"You have my cake. I paid good money for that."

She pushed the screen door open and handed him the box. "Enjoy it."

"To do that, I'd need a fork," Mac said.

With a soft curse, Emma spun and headed for the kitchen. She wasn't surprised to find him seated at her dining room table when she returned, the cake sitting in front of him. She handed him the fork, then took a seat at the other end of the table.

"Aren't you going to join me?" Mac asked.

"It's your cake," she said.

"Come on," he said. "I can't eat the whole thing."

Reluctantly, she moved down to the chair beside him and watched as he took the first bite. His eyes lit up and he smiled as he slowly swallowed. "That's a good cake," he said. "That's really delicious."

"Thanks," she said, feeling a flood of satisfaction.

"Worth every penny."

Emma shook her head. "That auction was so much fun. Too bad you guys didn't have your dueling pistols with you. You could have whipped them out and provided the whole town with even more to gossip over."

"It wasn't that bad. There was a lot at stake. The cake. My ego. Your heart."

Mac held out the fork to her and she ate the bite of cake perched on it. "It is good," she admitted.

He grinned and a shiver skittered down her spine. Even dripping wet, he was gorgeous. She reached out and wiped a bit of frosting from the corner of his mouth, then licked it off her finger.

Mac smeared frosting on her bottom lip, then leaned over and kissed her, his tongue taking care of the sweet mess on her mouth. Emma shuddered and drew a ragged breath, her gaze fixed on his.

"You're determined to do this, aren't you," Mac murmured.

Emma shook her head. "If you're not going to take care of it, then I'll find someone else. Maybe Charlie—"

"All right. If I agree, then we have to follow my rules," Mac said.

"What rules?"

"I get to…call the shots. This is going to be your first time and it's something that you'll remember the rest of your life. I'm not going to screw it up and have you remembering me in a negative light. So, we do it my way or we don't do it at all. Can you agree to that?"

"It seems a bit dictatorial, don't you think?"

"I'm not saying you can't enjoy it," Mac said. "Because you will. But I'm in charge."

Emma considered the offer for a long moment. When would she get another chance? He was willing and all she had to do was go along for the ride. How hard could that be? "All right, you're in charge."

She stood up and began to walk to the bedroom, stripping off her wet clothes and letting them drop to the floor along the way. But Mac continued to enjoy his cake, glancing over at her every now and then. When Emma was left in just her bra and panties, she stood at the bedroom door and waited for him to make the next move.

Groaning inwardly, she walked back to him, grabbing her clothes. "Sorry," she murmured. "I should have waited for *permission* to undress."

Maybe she shouldn't appear quite so enthusiastic. After all, didn't most men like women who played a bit hard to get? She glanced down at her shirt, tempted to pick it up and put it back on. But she couldn't bring herself to admit her fears.

"No, it's just that I enjoy that part," he said. "It's like unwrapping a present. You don't want someone else to jump in and spoil the anticipation."

"Do you want me to get dressed again?" To her consternation, he didn't seem anxious to carry on. She rubbed the goose bumps on her arms. "I'm kind of cold."

Mac shook his head. "We'll have to warm you up, then," he said. He slowly stood and shrugged out of his jacket. Then, he wrapped his hands around her waist and gently pushed her back against the edge of the table.

Emma's eyes fluttered and she waited for him to

kiss her. But instead, he reached out and scooped up a bit of frosting on his fingers, wiping a streak from the base of her neck to her belly.

Emma gasped in shock, but then he began to lick along the path he'd drawn, kissing and nipping her skin, setting her nerves on fire. She held her breath as wild sensations coursed through her body.

Her pulse raced and her blood began to warm, acting like a drug. Nuzzling her face into his damp hair, she took in the faint scent of his cologne on his shirt and smiled. Emma usually didn't care for cologne on men, but there was something about this scent that she found intriguing. If she stripped him naked, would his bare skin smell this way—of citrus and sandalwood?

"You must be cold, too," she said. Emma reached for the buttons on his shirt but he captured her wrists with his hands and held them behind her back. "You don't get to touch," he said.

"What?"

"You heard me. Just relax and enjoy. That's all you need to do right now. I don't want to have to tie you up."

Emma laughed. "You wouldn't tie me up!"

"My rules," he said. Mac stripped out of the shirt and tossed it aside, but when she reached for him, he grabbed her wrists again. "No touching."

He shifted and she watched the muscles bunch beneath his skin, fascinated.

He explored every inch of her torso with his lips and tongue. Tugging aside the silky fabric of her bra, his lips found her nipple and a groan slipped from her throat as he brought it to a hard peak.

Mac moved to the other side, tugging at the bra until

both breasts were completely exposed. Emma continued to watch him, as if she was standing outside her own body and observing the seduction of a stranger. This was finally happening and it all felt so good, but it was nothing like she'd thought it would be.

She imagined she'd be lulled into a haze of passion, a dreamy state where everything happened in slow motion. Instead, she was hyperalert, every nerve on fire, every sensation sharp and powerful. She couldn't relax, but that didn't matter.

Mac pushed her down onto the table, pulling her leg up along his hip and burying his face in the valley between her breasts. Emma wanted to run her fingers through his hair, to touch his face, but he'd made the rules very clear and she'd agreed to abide by them.

His fingers splayed across her belly, then slid lower, slipping beneath the waistband of her panties. He found the damp spot between her legs and began a gentle massage. Emma knew what an orgasm was and had helped herself to plenty of them. But the experience of a man's touch was beyond anything that she'd fantasized.

Every ounce of her attention was focused on the spot where his touch urged her forward. Emma wanted to let go, to surrender. She arched against him, breathless, aching for the torture to end. And yet, she couldn't seem to take that last step over the edge.

She'd watched enough movies and read plenty of books. She knew what to do and when to do it. The problem was, she'd never actually seduced a man. Just as she understood the basic mechanics of swimming, but she'd never make it across a small lake. She'd flipped through books about juggling, but could barely catch one ball and never three. Theoretical knowledge was nothing next to real-world experience!

As if he sensed her distress, Mac leaned close and whispered quiet encouragement to her, his breath warm against her ear. Emma closed her eyes and let the sound of his voice lull her into a delicious state of anticipation.

He continued to whisper his thoughts and desires, telling her what would happen if she just let go. And then it began, a pulse deep inside her that grew quicker with every breath she took. She couldn't focus her mind on anything but the pleasure that his touch was bringing.

She danced on the edge for a long time and it was only after he slipped his finger inside her that she surrendered to the inevitable. The first spasm took her by surprise and the rest, so powerful and shattering, stole her breath away.

As her orgasm faded, Emma was left with only one realization. She had no idea how sex with a man would feel. Her release at Mac's hands came as both a surprise and a stunning revelation.

An orgasm was definitely better with two.

MAC GRABBED THE bottle of wine from the fridge, then found a pair of wineglasses in the cabinet beside the sink. He walked back through the house to the bathroom. Emma was already submerged in the tub, the bubbles and hot water up around her chin.

"Is this what you wanted?" he asked, holding up the bottle.

"That will do," she said. "Can you pour me a glass?"

He did as she asked, then sat down on the floor across from the tub, stretching his legs out in front of him. He filled his own glass, then took a sip and sighed, his head falling back against the wall.

"Can I ask you something?"

Mac opened his eyes and met her gaze. "Sure."

"Why didn't we…finish?"

"We did," he said.

"But we didn't have sex."

"I don't think you were really ready. I want us to take our time. Get more comfortable with each other. We only just met. You might not like me once you get to know me."

"I like you now," she said.

"How is that possible? We're polar opposites, Em."

"Sometimes opposites attract," Emma said.

Mac had never really believed in that old adage. It was difficult enough to make a relationship work when the couple shared common interests. But he reminded himself that Emma didn't want a relationship. For her purposes, she wanted a man she could use then easily discard. There'd be no guilt or regrets that way. He'd insisted on setting the rules, but she was still in control.

"You're watching me take a bath," she said. "How much more comfortable with me do you need to be?"

"It's not me I'm worried about," he said with a smile. "Don't you want to enjoy yourself the first time you do it?"

Emma laughed. "No one enjoys it the first time. Everyone has strange stories. I want my strange story, too."

"You don't think this whole arrangement is a little

strange?" He took another sip of his wine. "Tell me something about yourself, Emma. Something that no one else in the world knows."

"I haven't led a very interesting life," she murmured. Emma drew a ragged breath. "I've…I've never been on an airplane." She covered her face with the washcloth. "I realize that sounds ridiculous in this day and age. Babies fly on planes. Grandmothers fly on planes. But not me."

"Why not?"

"When I was a kid, we didn't have money for vacations. And after that, I guess it started to turn into a phobia."

"You're afraid of flying?"

"I think I'm more afraid of freaking out in the airport or on the plane and humiliating myself. Or maybe I'm afraid of tumbling out of the sky and crashing to the ground? I just don't see the upside in getting into a plane, besides the destination."

"You realize I own a plane," Mac said.

"Yes," she said, giggling. "And though I'm sure you're a very competent pilot, there's no way I'd go up in a small plane."

"Have you ever thought about getting help?" he asked. "There are classes and books. Really good drugs. And liquor."

Emma shook her head. "The fear is pretty firmly embedded by now."

"So, no vacations outside the continental US?"

"I want to have adventures. I always dreamed of strolling down the Champs-Élysée, or watching the bulls run in Pamplona. But that's not my life. So no spontaneous shopping trips to New York. No wing-walking for the annual air show. No jetting off to Gstaad for the ski season."

"Maybe I should take you up sometime. I'm an excellent pilot," Mac said.

Mac thought about his own secrets. He had too many of them, and he'd kept them for so long. He'd never trusted anyone enough to talk about his past. But here, with Emma, he felt that he could say anything. In the short time that he'd known her, Mac had learned that Emma was fiercely loyal and fair-minded. She was also honest and thoughtful. "I don't have a passport," Mac said.

"That's not a big deal," Emma said. "I don't have one, either. But that shouldn't be surprising since I never go anywhere."

"I don't have a passport because I don't have a birth certificate. Actually, I do have one, somewhere. I just have no idea where."

"Where do you come from?" she murmured.

"That's the million-dollar question. I have no clue who I am or what my real name is."

She pushed up, bracing her arm on the edge of the tub. "You're Luke MacKenzie."

"I call myself Luke MacKenzie," Mac said. "But that's not my real name. That's what my social security card says, but the court issued that when I was sixteen. Same with my driver's license." He drew a deep breath. "I've never told that to a single person."

"You can trust me," she said. "What do you know about your childhood?"

Mac wasn't sure he ought to go on. Once she knew

the whole truth, it would change how she looked at him. She might change her mind about him, about their arrangement. She might question her decision to give up her virginity to someone who didn't know who he really was. And he had to remember that this thing between them was very temporary.

Mac closed his eyes and continued. He wanted to trust her, to take the chance that none of it would matter. Emma was different. "Some of what I'm going to tell you is true and some might be only what I imagine to be true. Many of my memories are foggy and out of focus. I know I had a father and a mother and we lived a rootless life. I suspect they were grifters. Petty criminals. We moved around a lot, usually living in motels or campgrounds. But sometimes apartments and houses. That never lasted long because money was always a problem."

"Did you go to school?"

"Occasionally. But as soon as someone started demanding my records from my previous school we were usually gone. For the most part, my mother taught me. She loved reading. We spent a lot of time at the library, reading. We never checked out books, though."

"Why not?"

"There would be no way to return them if we had to run. And a library card required identification, an address, a phone number."

Emma thought about that for a long moment and smiled. "Now I understand," she murmured. "There's a girl who comes to the library—she's a foster child. She never takes books home, even though I gave her a card. She's afraid they'll move her and she won't be able to get the books back."

"It's kind of odd. My mother and I lived off the profits of criminal activities, but we refused to break the rules of the local library."

"It sounds like you loved your mother."

"I did. But in the end, she left me for him. Even though he used to beat her and humiliate her, she went with him and left me behind."

"What happened?"

"I was twelve. We were staying in some trashy motel outside Denver, I think. It was snowing that night, really hard, and we had to pull off the road because we couldn't drive. My parents had a huge fight and I locked myself in the bathroom. When I woke up the next morning, they were gone."

"They just left you there?"

Mac nodded. "I waited for them to come back but after a couple of days, the motel manager came looking for the rent and found me. He called the cops and I ended up in the foster care system."

"Did they find your parents?"

Mac shook his head. "Nope. I'm sure they're out there somewhere, but I don't want to see them." He paused. "But I do have this box of stuff that my mother gave me when I was ten. She never let my father see the box, and she told me it held all my secret treasures. There are pictures of people in the box who I don't know. I wonder if they may be her parents. My grandparents."

"Did you ever think that you might have been kidnapped?" Emma asked.

"When I was a kid, I used to go through all the possibilities. But then, after they left, I just decided that my life was in the present and I had to stop dwelling on the past. I left it behind."

"And you're not curious now?"

He shook his head. "Nope. I mean, it would be nice to have passport. And I could apply to get one through the courts, but it would take lawyers and lots of money. I can live without."

"You really are a man of mystery. I like that."

"So does it make you think differently of me?" he asked.

Emma shook her head. "No. It makes me admire you more, that you were able to rise above that childhood and make something of yourself."

"I didn't have much of a choice," he murmured.

Mac was suddenly awash in doubts. He'd done what he swore he'd never do—talk about his past. He'd understood the risks, and yet, it had been so easy to tell it all to Emma. And she found it all so sexy. Would she feel that way once she realized how deep the scars ran?

He was the first one to admit that he still carried around a lot of baggage from his childhood. Yes, he was a man of mystery, but he had no interest in finding the answers to his past. He simply wanted to leave it behind him.

She couldn't fly without freaking out. He couldn't sleep in a hotel room. He couldn't commit to a relationship. He had no idea what love was, and had no intention of putting that much control in someone else's hands. He didn't make plans beyond the next few days.

And his solution to every problem in his present life was to simply walk away and make it part of his past.

Mac got to his feet, then set his wineglass on the edge of the sink.

"I should go," he said. "I've got an early day tomorrow."

"You could stay," Emma countered.

Mac shook his head. "I'll call you. We'll go out. Maybe next time we'll actually have a meal." He walked through the doorway, then turned back to find her watching him from the bath, a confused expression on her beautiful face. "Good night, Emma."

"Good night," she said.

As he walked out into the darkness, Mac reran their conversation in his head. Though he did trust her, it had been a risk to reveal so much to her. For now, his secrets made him seem mysterious and sexy. But there might come a time when they made him look broken and flawed, when they'd be used as an excuse for her to walk away, and leave him behind.

His body was covered with thousands of scars, shallow, invisible to the eye. These were the scars he'd inflicted on himself every day trying to hide the deeper secrets, the wounds inflicted when he was too young to protect himself. The man on the outside was sexy and charming and smart. It was the man on the inside who was a mess.

4

Lily Harper stood at the circulation desk, waiting patiently while Emma took care of another library patron.

"Hello, Miss Harper, what can I do for you today? Are you going to check out a book?"

Lily shook her head. "I—I was hoping you'd help me find something different."

"That's what I'm here for," Emma said. "What are you looking for?"

She glanced around nervously, hesitant to speak. Emma had seen this behavior before—from younger boys who wanted *National Geographic* magazines, to teenagers searching for *The Joy of Sex* or *The Kama Sutra*. Emma had made it a policy to always provide information when it was requested and to never censor or judge.

"Tell me what you want and I'll help you find it."

"I—I want to find my mother," she said. "They took me away from her when I was a baby and no one will tell me who she is or where she is. I'm twelve years old and I deserve to know. I—I have rights."

Though she'd always adhered to her policy, Emma wondered if it might backfire on her with Lily. From what she'd heard, Lily's foster family was planning to adopt her. It was their decision whether to give Lily more information about her mother, wasn't it? This might be an instance where Emma shouldn't interfere.

"Do you know anything about her?" Emma asked.

Lily shook her head. "Just what the social workers and my foster parents have told me. They said she was young and couldn't take care of me properly. She got in trouble with the police and had to go to jail." Lily paused. "But I'm not sure if that's true."

"Somewhere out there are the answers to all your questions. I can't guarantee they're here in the library, though, Lily." Emma turned to the computerized card catalog and typed in a few search terms. She found a book on adoptees trying to find their birth parents and wrote down the ID number.

"Let's check this out," she said.

Lily trailed after her as they walked upstairs to the adult nonfiction section. They wove through the stacks, and Emma realized that for the first time today, her mind wasn't on Mac. After their erotic intimacies the day before, Emma was left to wonder when they'd continue.

From the moment she'd opened her eyes that morning, her thoughts had fixed on him and the hours they'd spent together the night before—and in particular on the delicious thrill of her orgasm at his hands. She wanted to repeat the experience again and again, but she wasn't sure what Mac had planned.

In truth, once they'd actually had sex, it would be

all over. His task would be finished and they'd both move on. She'd made it very clear that she didn't expect anything more than that. But now that they'd started, Emma was forced to admit that sex was probably not something she would easily forget. If the actual sex was as wonderful as the orgasm she'd had, then it would be etched indelibly in her memory forever.

She drew a ragged breath. Maybe she ought to find a way to secretly videotape it. Then, after it was over, she could remember it exactly the way it was, kind of like pictures one might take on a vacation or at a special celebration.

Emma found the book for Lily and flipped through it, before handing it to her. "You could probably start with this," she said. "But I would also ask your foster parents if they'd help you. And your social worker. Let them know that you want to learn more about your real parents."

"I—I can't," Lily said. "This has to be a secret."

"Why?"

"Because they won't want me anymore. And I like living with the Prentisses. They're nice to me. I don't want them to hate me."

"I doubt they'd ever hate you, Lily," Emma said.

The girl handed the book back to Emma. "I should probably forget this. If my mother wanted to find me, she would have tracked me down by now."

Lily turned and walked out of the stacks, her footsteps fading as she walked down the stairs. Emma glanced down at the book. Wasn't there something she could offer the little girl? For someone her age, the task of finding her mother must seem impossible.

Emma paged through the book, her mind wandering to the conversation she'd had with Mac about his parents. He was in the same situation, abandoned without a clue. But his case was made even more difficult by parents who'd seemed to live off the grid.

When she got downstairs, she sat down behind her computer and began an internet search, scanning advice blogs and information services. It was all there for Lily to follow. She'd just have to post her story on some of the larger forums and see if anyone answered.

She lingered on a page that discussed DNA analysis by a genealogy service and how that might be useful for adoptees. As she read about the process, Emma began to believe that it was the perfect choice for Mac.

All that was required was a DNA swab from the inside of a person's cheek. The DNA would be analyzed and then matched to others in the database, who had given their consent to be identified. The matches would be revealed, and it was up to the subjects to make the connections and figure out the relationships. If there was someone in this database who was a match to Mac, it would at least give him a starting point.

Emma printed off the information and decided she'd offer it up to him that evening. She didn't want to push him, but she couldn't help but wonder what secrets his past might reveal. She was curious about the man in her life. And yet, she understood that he'd chosen to be cautious. He still carried a lot of the fears he'd developed as a child.

Emma smiled as she thought about how much their relationship had changed since that first meeting. They'd both been alone in the world, no family and few friends. But now they had each other. Maybe, after this was all over, they could remain friends.

She glanced at her watch. It was nearly lunchtime. She could pick up a few sandwiches and take them out to the airstrip and tell him about the DNA test. It was a good excuse to see him again.

As she gathered her things, Emma wondered if maybe she was acting a bit desperate. She'd decided to leave the details of their arrangement to Mac. He'd call her when he was ready to proceed to the next step. But not everything between them had to be about sex, right?

"I'm going to get some lunch, Kelly," she said as she walked to the front door. "I'll be back about one."

She stopped at the market and took far too long picking out the perfect elements for a picnic lunch—roast beef sandwiches on a baguette, a jar of Italian olives, some gourmet potato chips, two perfectly ripe pears and a wedge of cheese. She tossed in a pair of black cherry sodas, then hurried through the checkout line.

As she drove out to the airstrip, she couldn't help but wonder how they'd greet each other. Would he smile and kiss her cheek? Or would there be no acknowledgment of the passion they'd shared? Or maybe he would drag her into his arms and kiss her until her body went limp and her mind turned to mush....

Emma found him in the office, his feet kicked up on the desk, his nose buried in an old copy of *Sports Illustrated*. "I come bearing lunch," she said, holding up the bags.

Mac peeked over the edge of the magazine, then tossed it aside. "This is a nice surprise," he said.

Emma crossed the room and sat down at the desk, then began to unpack the bags. "I have another surprise, too. This one is even better."

"Better than you and black cherry sodas? That's going to be hard to beat."

She finished spreading the lunch out on the surface of the battered desk, then looked up at him. "What if you could find out the truth about your parents?" Emma asked. "Would you be curious?"

He thought about her question for a long moment. "If I could know, just know and that's all, maybe I'd want to. But I'm afraid of what else might come along with that information."

"What if you discovered your grandparents instead? Or your cousins? An aunt or uncle?"

"I've always thought that it was better to just let sleeping dogs lie," Mac said. He grabbed a sandwich and unwrapped it. "Roast beef?"

Emma nodded and reached for the potato chips, ripping the bag open and setting it in front of him. "I found a service that does DNA testing for genealogy purposes, and—"

"No," Mac said. "Thanks, but no. I don't want the government to have my DNA."

"This isn't the government or the police. It's a private company. They keep a database and try to match up people through their genealogies. I ordered a kit for you and they're going to send it to me."

"Emma, I said no!" His voice was sharp, his expression tense. He shook his head, then put his sandwich down. "I appreciate your interest, I really do. But I'm fine not knowing. I'm *better* not knowing." Mac placed his palms on the desk. "Actually, I'm really not that hungry right now. I've got a lot of work to do. I'll talk to you later."

He shoved his chair back and strode to the door. Cursing softly, Emma watched him leave, stunned at the sudden turn in his mood. She fought the urge to run after him, but she was determined not to appear too desperate. "I'm just trying to give you information."

When he reached the door, he spun around to face her. "But it's more than that, isn't it? You're worried what people are going to think if you give away your virginity to some bum. It's going to make you look bad."

"That's ridiculous," she said.

"I don't need your information. You can keep it. I'm not interested in finding my parents or grandparents or any other relatives I might have. I'm fine on my own." He walked outside and slammed the door behind him.

"No one should be alone in the world if they don't have to be," she murmured.

Emma waited for him to come back, but a few minutes later, she heard his truck start and then roar off down the road. She groaned softly, then grabbed her sandwich and took a big bite.

Obviously, sexual experience with a man didn't help her understand the opposite sex any better than she had before. Men were a mystery to her. But it was a mystery she was determined to untangle.

MAC TOOK THE steps of the library two at a time. He'd deliberately waited until just minutes before they closed, hoping that he'd be able to convince Emma to come out with him.

He'd behaved badly when she'd come to see him a few days ago. Emma had no idea what thinking about his past cost him. He'd always tried to be a positive kind of guy, but looking back brought a dark cloud over him that he felt compelled to fight off. It was his problem and he'd blamed her for it.

Pulling the heavy door open, he stepped inside. There was a small group of people gathered around the circulation desk, making their last-minute check-outs. When the crowd cleared, he caught Emma's gaze and waved at her.

She grabbed a few things from the desk, then walked over to him. "You're a little late. We close in two minutes."

"I know," he said. "I didn't come here for books. I came to apologize."

"For what?"

"For snapping at you the other day."

She frowned. "You snapped at me? I don't remember that."

"Over the DNA test. And I want you to know that I wasn't angry with you."

"I wouldn't have cared if you were," she said. "You're entitled to your own feelings when it comes to something like that. I understand."

Mac frowned. "You do?"

Emma nodded. "Sure."

He ought to feel relieved. But instead, Mac was a bit confused. Was she reacting like this because he didn't matter? This whole arrangement between them made things complicated at best. On the surface, they seemed to be having a romantic and sexual relationship. But then, it was also nothing more than an arrangement—one that would end the moment they had sex.

"I brought the stuff along," he said, reaching into his jacket pocket and pulling out a sheaf of papers.

"And I got the kit in the mail today," Emma said. "They move fast. Are you sure about this?"

"I decided you were right. Information isn't a bad thing," he said. "How does it work?"

"You just take a swab of the inside of your cheek and send it in. If anyone else in the system matches your DNA, they send their genealogical information and you have to figure out how you are connected. Or you might hear nothing. But they keep your information on file forever, so you could always have a match down the road."

He reached out and smoothed his palm over her cheek. "And what if I find out something bad?"

"You're the best man I know, Mac. Nothing will change my opinion of you." She pushed the papers back at him, and dropped the test kit on top. "Do it at home. Whenever you want to. It's up to you."

Mac shoved the papers and the kit into his pocket, then looked around. "Can I help you close?"

"Sure," she said. "This place is always kind of spooky once everyone leaves. The last librarian claimed we had a ghost, but I haven't seen any proof."

Over the next ten minutes, the last of the library patrons wandered through the lobby and out the doors. Emma locked them and walked toward him. "Alone at last," she murmured.

Mac couldn't read her mood. Though her words sounded lighthearted, her tone was a bit tense. "I've been thinking about our agreement," he said.

"Me, too," Emma replied. "It's just not working for me. I'm not a patient person. I've been waiting a long time and I don't want to wait any longer, so—"

"And I've been thinking that the agreement takes all the spontaneity out of things."

"I can understand if you want out, if you have doubts. Because I'm not sure—"

"No," Mac said. "I'm just saying that we should make a few revisions."

She walked over to the desk and began to remove books from the return bin, stacking them on a book cart beside her. "I'm listening."

"Maybe I don't have to be completely in charge. I want you to have some control, too."

After the lunch debacle, Mac had thought a lot about what they were doing. He'd been with a lot of women, but he'd never met anyone like Emma. She was so honest and direct, and she never seemed to judge him. Emma accepted him for the man he was. So why not give this budding relationship a fighting chance?

He'd always been in complete control in the past, hoping to protect himself. But, like the DNA test, maybe he was also denying himself the opportunity to have something great. It was time to trust a little more, and he couldn't think of a better person to trust than Emma.

Emma slowly turned. "So, if I wanted to do it right here and now, you'd be all right with that?"

He glanced around. "Sure. This would be fine."

She slowly strolled over to him. "All right." She smoothed her hand down the center of his chest. "So, if I want to kiss, I don't need your permission?"

"Correct," Mac said.

She leaned into him and Mac thought she was about to take advantage of her new freedom. But the instant before her lips brushed against his, she drew back. "Good to know. Although, I'm not sure what to do with all that power."

With a low growl, Mac reached out and wrapped his arm around her waist, pulling her body against his. His mouth covered hers in a demanding kiss, his tongue teasing until she opened beneath his assault. "You could try something like this," he said.

Emma's body went soft in his arms and he continued the kiss, creating a damp trail between her mouth and the base of her throat. She placed her hand on his chest then slowly undid the buttons on his shirt. When they were open to his waist, she ran her palms across his skin.

Drawing a quiet breath, she pressed a kiss to the center of his chest. Her lips were warm and damp and Mac closed his eyes and enjoyed the effects of her kisses as they heated his blood and made his pulse quicken.

His fingers tangled in her hair and he drew her back up to his mouth, desperate to taste her. She was sweet and addictive, like a fine wine. The more he kissed her, the drunker he felt, as if each taste went right to his head.

Mac had expected her to be a bit shy or reserved when it came to taking the lead, but Emma seemed perfectly happy to plunge forward. In truth, he found her breathless enthusiasm very sexy.

She reached for his belt buckle and undid it, then pulled the belt from around his waist. It snapped and the end hit her in the face.

"Ow." She rubbed the spot with her fingertips and Mac leaned forward to kiss it, chuckling softly.

"You're dangerous," he murmured.

"I've learned all my romantic moves from the movies," she said. "I've studied very hard for this moment."

"What are you planning to do?" he asked.

She grabbed his hand and pulled him along to her office. After she shut the door behind them both, she reached for the venetian blinds and closed them. A sigh of relief slipped from her throat when she was finished.

He wandered around the office and examined a shelf full of crazy hats, picking up a pith helmet and putting it on his head. "Nice," he said, facing her.

"They're for story time," she said, putting the hat back on the shelf. "They add to the adventure." She smiled nervously. "I've never done this before. You'll tell me if I'm doing something wrong?"

He nodded, and with trembling fingers, she unbuttoned his jeans and slowly drew the zipper down. Being aware that this was her first time made the anticipation even more acute. Mac held his breath as she slipped her hand inside his jeans and began to stroke him. He was already hard. He watched the expression on her face—at first startled and then delighted.

He couldn't imagine what was going through her mind but it didn't matter once she bent down in front of him. Mac closed his eyes and leaned back against the counter as she took him into the damp warmth of her mouth.

"You're better at this than you know," he murmured, gently brushing the hair from her face.

She began slowly, tentatively, as if she was afraid she was going to hurt him. But as her movements became more determined and his pleasure more intense, her skill grew exponentially.

As he came closer to the edge, Mac tried to control his response. When the end was just an instant away, he drew Emma to her feet and kissed her, her fingers taking him the rest of the way.

His breath caught in his throat and he groaned as the spasms sapped the strength from his limbs. The orgasm seemed to last forever, spinning out in a riot of intense sensation. He held on to her, clutching her backside as he found release in her touch.

"Was that all right?" she whispered.

"It was perfect," he said. "You must be a very quick study."

Emma smiled. "I knew what to do in theory, but until I actually did it, I wasn't sure if what I knew was right."

"Was it what you expected?" he asked, pressing a kiss to the curve of her neck.

"Not at all. You were really hard. And hot. But soft, too, like silk. It was very…enlightening."

"I'm glad I could be of help," Mac said.

She drew away and looked into his eyes. "I'll never be able to thank you for this," she said. "I realize it sounds silly, but you're exactly the person I needed.

Someone patient and kind and undemanding. You're the perfect one."

Mac pulled her into his embrace. His worst fear was that this would all end with an act that usually meant a beginning. How could he walk away from Emma after finally enjoying every pleasure that her body offered?

Mac knew he shouldn't raise his expectations. He'd understood what this was from the beginning and he'd gladly accepted his role. But the closer he and Emma became, the more he realized what a good match they were. For the first time in his adult life, he wanted to put down roots, to live a life that revolved around loving rather than leaving.

And yet, a tiny shard of doubt worried him, like a sliver of glass beneath his skin. Would this feeling last? Or would it fade once the initial infatuation wore off? It was easy to be madly in love, living in a world where passion was all he cared about. What would happen when the drudgery of day-to-day life took over—when worries about work and finances replaced thoughts of passion?

Maybe it was best to stick to the plan. He was due to leave San Coronado early next month. Buddy would be back and he'd be out of a job. And as he'd done so many times before, he'd move along, searching for another spot to park his plane.

He was happy now, in this very moment, and that would have to be enough.

"MY NEPHEW WILL be coming to town next weekend," Leonora Brady said as she put her books into the canvas bag she'd brought along. "He's a pharmacist. Excellent prospects, if I do say so. I wondered if you might like to come to dinner. I'll make my famous stuffed peppers."

"Next weekend?" Emma asked. "I'll have to check my calendar."

"Did I mention he's very handsome? He looks a bit like a young Tony Bennett."

"The singer?"

"Yes, although I don't believe he can sing."

"I'll get back to you."

Leonora hefted her bag up over her shoulder. "You'd love him."

Emma watched as the older woman walked to the front entrance. Regina Farley took her place, setting a stack of books on CD onto the counter. "I've seen the boy. He looks like an *old* Tony Bennett, toupee and all. *My* nephew, however, is exactly the kind of man you'd love. His name is Warren and he's a CPA. He has his own practice in Sacramento. Mainly taxes. And he owns his own home. We see him every Sunday for dinner. Perhaps you could join us next week?"

"Thank you for the invitation, but I'm typically quite busy on Sundays."

"I usually make a rolled rib roast," Regina said. "And roasted new potatoes and a lemon meringue pie." She reached out and patted Emma's forearm. "You just give me a call and let me know, dear."

Emma quickly checked out Regina's selections and then called up the next person in line. To her relief it was Trisha, who was loaded down with a stack of plays by Arthur Miller. "All done with Keats?" Emma asked.

"Yes," she said. "I see word is out that you and Charlie are officially over."

"I've had two offers already," Emma said. "A pharmacist and a CPA. I guess they haven't heard that I'm trying to sleep with the local crop duster."

"How's that going?" Trisha asked.

"We're getting there," Emma murmured. "Slowly."

"Isn't that the best way?" Trisha asked with a knowing grin.

Emma shivered at the memory of what had happened in her office the previous night. "It has been good. Very enlightening."

"Really?"

Emma nodded. "I'll tell you all about it later. It's going to take a bottle of wine and some privacy."

"Oh, great. I was hoping it would be fabulous. I mean, look at the man. He was clearly made for hot sex."

"I'm not sure the rest of the town will approve. I think I'm about to be barraged by suitable candidates."

"Maybe you should play the field," Trisha said. "I've got a cousin I could introduce you to. Your crop duster is going to head out of town soon and—" Trisha paused and searched Emma's expression. "Oh, Em, no. You can't possibly be hoping that—"

Trisha looked around and called to one of the assistant librarians, then took Emma by the arm and dragged her back to her office. She closed the door behind her. "Please tell me you're not falling in love with this guy."

"It's hard not to!" Emma cried. "It's a problem for women everywhere. For us, sex is romance and love.

For men, it's a physical release. Believe me, I keep reminding myself of that fact. And I know he'll be leaving. But I want to enjoy every moment of this. And if I fall a little bit in love, that's all right. I should cry a little bit when he leaves."

Trish held out her arms and gave Emma a fierce hug. "You're a big girl. I trust you. And I'm sure I don't have to give you a lecture on safe sex."

"We haven't had sex yet," she said. "But I will remember your advice."

Trisha grinned. "Good. I'm so happy for you. I know how much this means to you. And if it doesn't work out, I have a cousin who is moving to San Francisco and he's kind of hot."

"I'll keep that in mind," Emma said.

A knock sounded on her office door and Ann Marie popped her head inside. "Denise Prentiss would like to speak to you. Can I send her in?"

"Sure," Emma said. She rolled her eyes at Trisha. "She probably has a second cousin who's an acupuncturist."

"I'll call you later," Trisha said as she slipped out.

A moment later, another figure appeared in the doorway. Emma held out her hand. "Mrs. Prentiss. What can I do for you?"

Denise Prentiss held out a book. "I was hoping you could explain this," she said. "I found it in Lily's backpack."

Emma glanced down at the book. It was the one she'd suggested to Lily about adoptees finding their birth parents. "I didn't realize she'd checked it out." Emma smiled. "That's a big step for her."

Denise scowled, then set the book on Emma's desk. "How dare you give her a book like that. What were you thinking? I'm sure you're aware of our situation. This is a difficult time for everyone and you're making it even worse by encouraging Lily to find her mother. This is none of your business. You've overstepped your responsibilities as our town librarian. I will be lodging a complaint with the library board."

Emma was stunned at the anger in Denise Prentiss's expression. She'd always been a very cool and calm person. "Lily came to me looking for answers. It has always been my policy not to judge. And I did advise her to talk to you about her questions." Emma paused and motioned to a chair. Denise sat down and Emma took the chair next to her. "Were you aware that Lily spends every day after school alone at the library? And that she refuses to check out any books? She reads her books and then puts them back on the shelf every day when she's done."

"She said she was staying late at school for extra help with her homework," Denise said. She shook her head. "I don't understand. I wouldn't care if she wanted to go to the public library. Why would she lie to me?"

"I think she's afraid to disappoint you," Emma said. "You probably expressed some pleasure that she was staying late for extra help, and now she thinks if she doesn't continue, you'll be disappointed."

"That's ridiculous."

"It is. But Lily lives with a whole different set of fears than you and I do. And she can't always be rational about them."

"How do you know?"

"We've struck up a friendship. We talk."

Tear welled up in Denise's eyes. "I've tried with her, but she won't let me get close. I'm patient and understanding, but it's like running into a brick wall, day after day after day."

"How much information do you have about her mother?"

"She was fifteen when she had Lily. She got involved with drugs and prostitution and they found Lily left alone in a car. She was just a toddler. Since then, her mother has had more drug problems and she's been in and out of prison."

"Maybe you should share that with Lily," Emma said. "She has to fill in all the blank spaces in her life before she can start a new life with you."

"You're right," Denise said. "I thought I was protecting her, but the more I try, the more she pulls away." Denise stood. "I—I'm sorry to have disturbed you. I shouldn't have, I apologize. Thank you for taking the time with Lily and for listening to her concerns. And I won't be reporting you to the library board."

Emma nodded. "We have several good books about bringing up difficult subjects with children. If you give me a day, I can pull them for you. They might help."

Denise walked out of the office, closing the door behind her. Emma circled her desk and sat down in her chair. She rubbed at a tension headache that was beginning in her left temple and spreading over her forehead.

Lily was just a little girl and her life was already a tangle of irrational fears and self-protective lies. Emma couldn't imagine the snarl of emotions that Mac kept so well hidden. On the surface, he seemed like the perfect guy, so cool and in control. But there had to be scars that he was hiding, fears buried so deep that he couldn't excise them. Could she help him, or would she only make things worse?

Another knock sounded on her door and Emma groaned. What now? Another potential suitor? "Come in."

To Emma's shock, Charlie stood in the doorway, his arms crossed over his chest. "You owe me a cake," he stated coldly. "And it better be as good as the one you gave MacKenzie."

He turned and strode away and Emma laughed softly. She'd completely forgotten Charlie. Her life was becoming a giant soap opera and there was nothing she could do about it.

5

It was a perfect fall morning, the air crisp and cold, the dew thick on the grass in Emma's front yard. Mac strode up the front walk in the predawn light, his footsteps breaking the silence. After taking the front steps two at a time, Mac pressed the doorbell.

He heard the chimes through a nearby open window and a few seconds after that, Emma's voice calling through the house. When the front door finally swung open, Mac found her wrapped in a thick bathrobe, her dark hair tumbling around her sleepy face.

"What time is it? What are you doing here?" She raked her fingers through her hair. "It's cold out here. Come in." She reached out and grabbed his hand, tugging him inside. They started to head to the bedroom and Mac pulled her to a stop. "I need you to get dressed," he said. "I want to leave in fifteen minutes."

"Where are we going?" she asked.

"Mammoth Lakes," Mac replied. "I have to deliver a new swimming pool pump to a guy I know. There's a really great spot up there for breakfast. I thought we'd eat and I'd have you back in time for work. The library opens at noon today, right?"

She nodded. "Yes, but I'm not working today. I have to finish the budget for next year and I was going to go through my fourth-quarter book order." Emma started toward the bedroom, then stopped suddenly. "How are we going to get there? Mammoth Lakes is almost six—" She slowly turned. "You're not suggesting we *fly*, are you?"

"Yeah, that was the plan," Mac said. "I figured it was about time you faced your fears. I sent that DNA test in and—"

"You sent it in?" Emma threw her arms around him and gave him a tight hug. "I'm so proud of you. I know how difficult that was. Now, I don't want you to get your hopes up because—"

"I'm trying not to think about it too much," Mac said. "So maybe we can not talk about it?"

Emma nodded. "Sure, I understand." She pressed her finger to her lips.

"As I was saying, I faced my fear, now it's your turn to face yours." She looked confused. "Flying?" he clarified.

Emma's eyes went wide. "Oh, no, no, no. There's a huge difference between the two. You swabbed your mouth. I'm getting into a plane that could come hurtling down from the sky and crash into a million pieces." She shook her head. "I'm going back to bed. Have a nice trip."

Mac followed after her, flopping down on the bed after she'd crawled beneath the covers. He pulled her close and nuzzled her neck. "So you plan to be afraid of flying for the rest of your life?"

"No. I just think it's best to work on one problem at a time. And you know which problem you're assigned to," Emma said, her voice muffled by the pillow.

"Emma, look at me." He gently turned her to face him, then smoothed the hair away from her pretty face. "Do you trust me?"

"Of course I do."

"Then trust me on this. You'll be 100 percent safe. The weather is perfect. It's a short trip. If anything goes wrong, I can put the plane down on a country road or in a field."

"What could go wrong?" she asked.

"Nothing," Mac countered. "I promise, it will be an impeccable flight. And you might even enjoy yourself." He leaned closer and brushed a kiss across her lips. "Say yes," he whispered.

"No," she said, a stubborn set to her jaw.

He kissed her again, this time more intently. "Say yes," he repeated. "You have to put this fear behind you." Mac took her hand and gently pulled her out of bed. "I'll help you get dressed."

When she stood beside the bed, Mac stripped off the shapeless bathrobe. She wore flannel pajamas beneath. He skimmed the bottoms down over her hips, bracing a hand on her waist as she stepped out of them.

"Underwear?" he asked.

"Top drawer," she said, nodding toward the dresser. "Pick something nice. If I'm going to die today, I should be wearing pretty underwear when they find me."

"Some pilots might consider that an insult," he

said. "But since I get to pick through your underwear drawer, I'll blame it on your nerves."

He opened the drawer and was surprised to find such a riot of color tangled up inside. He found a pretty turquoise-blue bra and plucked out a pair of panties in bright magenta.

Mac brought them to the side of the bed and Emma scowled and shook her head. "Those don't match," she said.

"I don't care," Mac said, slipping the panties over her ankles. "I like these."

It was almost impossible to ignore the temptations that her naked body offered. Her skin was so smooth and warm, and he fought the urge to throw her back down on the bed and press his lips to the soft curves of her inner thigh. But he had plans for the day, and the first thing on the agenda was a plane ride. The rest would come later.

Her pajama top came next and Mac gathered his resolve, knowing that her breasts would be difficult to resist. He unbuttoned the front of her shirt then brushed the flannel off her shoulders. He caught himself holding his breath as his gaze skimmed over her torso.

She was incredibly beautiful, her body soft and feminine in a purely natural way. He leaned forward slightly, needing to capture a perfect, pink nipple between his lips. Just one taste would be enough. But Mac realized he was deluding himself. One taste would never be enough. With Emma, it was all or nothing.

Mac quickly stood and helped her into the bra, fastening it with nimble fingers.

"You're pretty good at that," she said, running her

fingers through her tangled hair. "Have you had a lot of practice?"

"I have a yearly subscription to the Victoria's Secret catalog," he said. "And I once removed a woman's underwear with my teeth."

She glanced over her shoulder. "Really?"

"No," Mac admitted. "But you were impressed for a moment, weren't you?"

Emma giggled. "Yes, I was. Maybe I'll let you try."

"I'll be sure to put that on our agenda." Mac wandered around her bedroom, gathering shirts and jeans for her to choose from, but she ignored them and found a clean pair of jeans and a pretty top in her closet.

"Speaking of our agenda," she said. "Am I allowed to ask when we're going to get to the matter at hand?"

"You may ask," Mac said. "But I'm not sure I'll have an answer. It's going to happen when it happens."

"But we have an agreement," Emma said. "It doesn't matter when it happens, as long as it happens. Soon."

He pulled the gauzy top over her head, then helped guide her arms into the sleeves. "Believe me, it makes a difference."

Emma grabbed the jeans and stepped into them, wiggling her backside until she could button and zip them. "We could do it right now. We could take off all our clothes, get into bed and be done with it."

"Sweetheart, let me assure you that when we do it, you're going to want it to go on forever. You're not going to be 'done with it.'"

"See? This is the problem. You're building it up to be something so wonderful that I'm sure I'm going to be disappointed."

"There is something to creating a little anticipation," he said.

"I've had at least fifteen years of anticipation. It's enough, believe me." She grabbed the front of his jacket and gave him a playful shake. "Please, promise me it's going to be soon. I can't wait much longer."

He slipped his hand around her nape and pulled her into a long, lingering kiss, his tongue slowly tracing the crease of her lips. "I promise," he said.

She slipped into her shoes then glanced around the room. "What else do I need?"

"A warm jacket. The heater in the plane doesn't work that well."

Her pretty expression transformed into one of reluctance. "I don't want to get in your plane."

"I could tie you to the wing," he said.

"Don't joke about that. I have nightmares about riding on the wing of a plane."

The sun was just peeking over the eastern horizon as they walked out of her house and got into his truck. Mac turned the key in the ignition and his truck rumbled to life. He pulled away from the curb and noticed the expression of dread on her face.

Maybe this wasn't such a great idea, he mused. He had no clue how deep her fear of flying went. He could answer all her questions, soothe all her doubts, explain exactly how the plane lifts off the ground and how it gently descends and lands, but what if she was still afraid?

"I think I know why you're doing this," she murmured.

"Why is that?"

"Because flying is a perfect metaphor for sex," she explained.

A long silence grew between them. "That's exactly right," Mac lied. "A metaphor."

In truth, he had other motives. Mac didn't want Emma to remember him solely as the guy who had taken her virginity. He wanted to be more than that—he wanted to be the man who introduced adventure and excitement into her life. Conquering her fear of flying would open up a whole new world to Emma. He wanted to be the man who gave that to her.

"So it's a metaphor for me. I understand how flying works, the same way I understand how sex works: theoretically. And now, I'm going to get some practical, real-life experience."

"And how does that metaphor work out if you have a complete breakdown and you refuse to go up in the plane?"

"I guess that wouldn't be a very good thing," Emma said. She looked over at him. "I think I'm going to have to get on that plane."

"READY?" MAC ASKED.

With white-knuckled hands Emma grasped the shoulder belts that Mac had clipped around her. Getting her inside the plane had taken nearly a half hour and the sun was now well above the horizon and shining directly into her eyes. Mac had done his preflight check three times just to please her and he'd explained the physics of flight in great detail.

The only thing left she could think of to stop the flight would be the need for a bathroom break. But

Emma was afraid that she'd lock herself inside the hangar bathroom and refuse to come out. "You promise we're going to be all right."

"I promise," he said, popping the headphones over her ears.

She closed her eyes, covering them with her hands and nodded. "Go, go, go," she said.

Emma heard the plane's engine power up and the wheels begin to bump along beneath her. Their speed increased and the clatter around her was almost deafening. It sounded as if the plane was about to fall apart around them.

As if he could read her mind, his voice came through the headphones. "Don't worry. It sounds worse than it is. Buddy's runway is pretty bumpy but this plane is one of the most sturdy and dependable in the air."

Somehow that didn't make her feel better. Emma felt a scream building in her throat. Then suddenly, the plane went quiet. She opened her eyes and glanced over at him. She expected them to be falling from the sky, but then she noticed the propeller spinning in front of them. They were in the air and slowly rising.

Emma swallowed hard, fighting back a flood of nausea. She was afraid to look out the side window, but when Mac banked the plane to the north, she had no choice.

"You all right?" he asked.

She nodded. "I think so."

"Take a few deep breaths," he said. "Then enjoy the ride."

Over the next hour and a half, they flew northeast over the rugged peaks and dense forests of the Sierra

Nevada mountains, broken only by a highway or river here and there. Though everything looked the same to Emma, Mac seemed to know exactly where they were going, and before long they were descending, making a lazy circle in the early morning light.

"See it?" he asked, pointing out her window.

Emma squinted. "I don't see anything."

"Cut out of that clearing. Right there."

Emma gasped. "We're landing there? But the strip is so short. And it's surrounded by trees."

"It's a little tricky, but I've landed on worse."

As they got closer to the ground, Emma's started to panic again. But this time, she reminded herself that Mac knew what he was doing. She trusted him against her own common sense. She had faith that he would protect her and keep her safe.

To Emma, it was a startling realization. The only person she'd ever really trusted was her mother. Since her death, she'd been on her own. But now she had Mac.

She didn't really have him, though, Emma mused. He was present in her life for the moment. But he wasn't the type to stick around. Luke MacKenzie was a drifter and he'd drift out of her life as quietly as he'd drifted in.

"Ladies and gentlemen, we're making our approach and will be on the ground in Mammoth Lakes in just a few minutes. Please make sure your belongings are stowed beneath the seat in front of you and your tray tables are up and seat belts fastened. And thank you for flying MacKenzie Air." He paused, then glanced over at her. "You may want to cover your eyes for this."

Emma did as she was told. Suddenly, the plane started to shake and shudder as it rolled down the runway. When it finally came to an abrupt stop, Emma pulled her hands back. "Did we make it?"

Mac reached over and wove his fingers through the hair at her nape. Then, he pulled her into a lazy kiss, his lips soft yet demanding. "Come on, I have a surprise for you."

"If you bring out a helicopter, I'm going to hate you forever."

"No," he said. "It's nothing like that." He grabbed her hand and wove his fingers through hers, helping her out of the plane.

A few moments later, a pair of Jeeps sped down the runway and stopped near the plane. Mac introduced Steve and Marlene Anderson, the proprietors of the High Sierra Resort and Spa.

Marlene motioned Emma toward her Jeep. "I'll take you up to the lodge and get you settled while Mac and Steve take care of the plane. I can't tell you how thankful we are for Mac. Our pool pump broke last night and he found one for us in Fresno and offered to fly it up here this morning."

"Have you known Mac for long?"

"Oh, five or six years. When we were renovating the resort, he flew supplies in and out for us. He bought the Beaver from Steven. How was your flight?"

"Fine," she said. "Just fine."

When the lodge came into view, Emma gasped. The sprawling log lodge was set against a beautiful backdrop of snow-covered peaks and deep green forest. "It's lovely," she said.

"We've put you in one of our lodge suites. It has a fireplace and a whirlpool tub."

"But we're not staying the night," Emma said.

"Yes, but you'll be here for the day and we want to make sure you are comfortable."

Marlene grabbed a key from behind the desk and walked with Emma to the elevator, stepping inside as the door opened. They rode up to the third floor. Marlene unlocked the door, then placed the key in Emma's hand. "I'll send up our spa concierge and you can choose anything off the menu, complementary, of course. Enjoy your stay."

"Thank you," Emma called, still confused by Marlene's offer. Why would they need a room if they were just going to have breakfast and then… "Leave?" she murmured.

Emma wandered into the room, taking in the luxurious appointments. She walked to the wall of windows and stared out at the mountains, a smile twitching at the corners of her mouth. It was gorgeous and so romantic! And she knew exactly why Mac had insisted upon it. This was where they were finally going to make love.

She paced across the room, then hurried to the bed and pulled the down comforter back. She wasn't going to let him get away this time. Emma shrugged out of her jacket and draped it over a dining chair in the living area of the suite.

Her nerves threatened to get the better of her and Emma searched for the room's minibar. She opened it and grabbed a small bottle of white wine. She felt a small measure of relief as she drank it straight out of the bottle. It was absolutely necessary that she relax, or Mac was going to find another excuse to put off them having sex.

She quickly stripped off her clothes, then looked at her mismatched underwear. How could she have missed the signs? He'd chosen the colors, a combination that he found sexy.

Her pulse began to pound and Emma drew a deep breath. He'd been so calm on the plane. She stared out the windows. Emma had always just assumed that they'd make love at night. Doing it in the middle of the day seemed a bit unconventional.

She crawled into the bed and tried to strike a casual pose. "Maybe he should come upon me naked in the tub," Emma murmured. "Or in the midst of a shower. That would be really sexy."

But she wasn't sure when he'd get to the room, so she could be in the shower for the next half hour. The bed would be best. In the end, she crawled between the crisp sheets without her underwear. He couldn't possibly misunderstand her intentions if she was completely naked.

Emma waited, watching the minutes tick by on the digital clock beside the bed. When there was finally a loud knock at the door, she was so nervous, she nearly jumped out of her skin.

"Just calm down," she murmured to herself. Emma slipped out of bed and hurried to the door. Taking a deep breath, she pulled the door open and struck a sexy pose, her leg wrapping provocatively around the edge of the door. "Didn't they give you a key?"

"Are you Miss Bryant?"

A young woman in a pale peach uniform stood outside in the hall, a tray in her hands. Emma quickly pulled her leg back inside. "I—I'm sorry," she said, peering around the door. "I was expecting someone else."

"Mr. MacKenzie is going to be a while. He's helping Mr. Anderson with the pool pump. My name is Heather. I've brought you mimosas. And Mr. MacKenzie thought you might enjoy a massage or one of the other spa services? I can arrange that for you."

"A massage?" Emma asked. She groaned inwardly. She'd never had a massage in her life. Was this supposed to be a part of the seduction? What if she refused?

"Actually, a manicure and pedicure might be nice. Do you do those?"

"I'll send up our aesthetician," Heather said.

"Good," Emma replied. "I'll be waiting. Just leave the tray next to the door."

As she closed the door, Emma felt her face warm with embarrassment. Maybe a mani-pedi would relax her. She laughed to herself. The only thing that would calm her nerves down now was a large glass of vodka followed by another large glass of vodka.

Emma slipped into one of the luxurious robes that hung on the bathroom wall, then hurried out to get the tray of champagne and orange juice. Mimosas would have to do for now.

MAC STOOD OVER the bed and stared down at a sleeping Emma. She was wrapped in one of the resort's complementary bathrobes, the neckline gaping to reveal the gentle swell of her left breast. A tiny pink crescent of her nipple peeked from beneath the open collar, and Mac's fingers twitched with the urge to touch it.

He glanced around the room and noticed the half-empty champagne bottle sitting on the table near the window. He walked over and grabbed the bottle and took a sip, then sat down on the edge of the table, his gaze skimming along her slender legs.

Her toenails were painted a bright shade of pink, and he noticed the same shade on her fingernails. Had she taken advantage of the massage, as well? If the massage hadn't put her to sleep, then the champagne had.

Mac considered letting her sleep. They had about four hours before they needed to head back. More than enough time to enjoy the room and all the amenities that resort had to offer.

He sank down on the edge of the bed, then leaned over and brushed a kiss across her lips. This would be the perfect place to take the final step in their carnal contract. He'd done his best to slow their progress, knowing that once it was over, he'd have no excuse to see her again.

But though his fears about the future were at war with his sexual desires, Mac wanted to make love to her, to feel that ultimate intimacy, to complete the circle that she was so determined to draw. He had to hope that it would be so good between them that once would not be enough for her.

"Emma?" he whispered, his lips pressed against her forehead. "Wake up, sweetheart."

She groaned softly, and it took another kiss before her eyes fluttered open. "I fell asleep," she said. Pushing up on her elbow, she looked around the room. "Oh, the mimosas." A smile curled her lips as she flopped back down. "I got my toes and fingers done, too."

"And a massage?"

"No, I wasn't in the mood for some stranger to rub my body. I wanted to leave that for you."

Mac reached out and ran a finger along the edge of robe lapel. "Would you like to stay here tonight? We can fly back tomorrow morning."

"Can we?"

"They gave us the room. And lunch. And dinner. But if you want to go home, we should leave by three. I can't land at Buddy's in the dark."

"What time is it now?"

"Eleven. We've got four hours to decide."

She smiled. "Why don't you grab one of these robes and join me?"

"I need to grab a quick shower first," he said. "I'm a little grimy from working on that pool pump."

Emma leaned back against the headboard, placing her foot in the center of his chest. "Make it quick, mister."

Mac jumped off the bed and began to discard his clothing as he walked to the bathroom. They'd been given a deluxe room and the shower was a wonder of technology. The showerhead was the size of a large pizza, and touch controls turned the water on and off.

When he'd shed the last of his clothes, Mac stepped beneath the warm water. He closed his eyes and tipped his face up. He waited, hoping that she'd follow him into the shower. When he felt her hand on his chest, Mac opened his eyes to meet her gaze. "I think this is going to be it," he murmured.

She held up a box of condoms. “Good. I’m sick of carrying these around everywhere I go.”

Mac chuckled and grabbed her waist, pushing her back against the wall of the shower as he pressed his body into hers. He skimmed his palm along her hip and down her thigh, then pulled her leg up around his hip. He was already hard and the tip of his shaft slipped along the warm crease between her legs.

Her arms snaked around his neck as she kissed him, her mouth desperate on his, demanding every ounce of his attention. Mac ran his hands through her hair, brushing the damp strands from her face as his lips met hers. He’d never forget the taste of her, the sweet warmth that he found so addictive.

She had become his salvation, the answers he’d searched for his entire life. The hard shell around his heart had been cracked, and with each kiss, the protection fell away. He’d been so careful, but somehow he’d forgotten all his rules the moment he first set eyes on Emma.

He’d never felt more powerful, nor more vulnerable than when he was with her. Was this a mistake? If his feelings for her ran so deep now, how would he feel after they made love? Would he be able to walk away?

Emma stepped back and pressed the sodden box of condoms to his chest. “I can’t wait any longer,” she murmured.

Mac smiled and dropped a kiss on her lips. “We have all afternoon,” he said.

“And we can do it again and again if you like. But I don’t want to bother with the foreplay. I—I just want to…”

"Say it, Em," he murmured. "Tell me what you want."

"I want to feel you move inside me. I want to know what it is to have you fill me up."

Mac nodded, then opened the box of condoms and handed one to her. "Have you read about what to do with this?"

She winced. "Yes. But I have no practical experience."

Mac helped her smooth it over the length of his stiff shaft. "Very good," he said, pressing a kiss to her temple.

"Thank you for being so patient with me."

Emma reached down and gently wrapped her fingers around him. Mac slipped his hands beneath her backside and picked her up, wrapping her legs around his hips. He was there, poised to slip inside her, but he waited.

Emma held her breath as she slowly lowered herself onto his erection. Mac wasn't prepared for the flood of pleasure that raced through his body as her warmth enveloped him. He groaned softly when she'd reached her limit, pressing his face into the curve of her neck.

Though he'd had his share of women and considered himself an experienced lover, everything felt different with Emma. He'd somehow taken on her vulnerabilities and her insecurities. It was as if it were his first time, as well.

Mac held her against the wall of the shower and slowly began to move, withdrawing with care before he plunged deeply. A moan slipped from her throat and he drew back, searching her expression for some sign of discomfort. But her eyes were closed and a tiny smile quirked at the corners of her lips.

He increased his rhythm, holding fast to her hips. Emma's fingers dug into his shoulders, but he didn't feel any pain, just the incredible sense of anticipation as his orgasm began to build. Mac wanted to bring her along with him, but she'd made it very clear what she wanted.

Still, he'd decided long ago to make their first time together memorable, and he wasn't going to disappoint. He held on to her as he brought her feet down to the floor, then turned her around.

Mac gently bit her shoulder as he entered her from behind. Reaching around, he began to caress her sex as he moved. Her response was immediate and intense. Emma cried out as if the rush of sensation he'd caused took her by surprise.

He could tell that he'd found her weakness and before long, she was gasping with each stroke. The water washed over them, the shower now filled with steam. Mac carefully controlled the tempo and, when he finally sensed her impending release, he gave her what she needed, pushing her over the edge.

Her body shuddered as the spasms took over. An instant later he joined her and he held on until the last wave of pleasure had subsided.

Mac grabbed her waist and pulled her out of the shower. He wrapped a clean robe around her, then dried her hair with a towel. "So?" he said. "Was it what you expected?"

Emma pulled the towel in front of her face, then ran out of the bathroom. He grabbed his own bathrobe and followed her, flopping down on the bed beside her. He pulled the towel away from her face. "You're blushing," he said.

Emma nodded. "It was…astonishing."

"Astonishing. That's good."

"Very good. Better than good. Excellent." She smiled. "Now I understand how people lose their minds over it. I mean, I want to do it again, and we just finished."

"No, we're just getting started," he said.

"We are?"

"Yes."

Emma giggled. "Perfect. Because there are a lot of things I'd really like to try."

"Theoretical things?" Mac asked.

"Yes."

"Maybe you better give me a list so that I can prioritize."

Emma rolled on top of him, pinning his hands above his head. "Why don't you just lie still and I'll do some experimenting."

Mac closed his eyes and smiled. This wouldn't be the last time with Emma. She wasn't going to walk away. For now, she was part of his life and he was going to enjoy every moment they had together.

6

EMMA HAD WATCHED a lot of Sunday-mornings-in-bed scenes. They were a staple in almost every romantic movie she'd watched. But she'd never expected to experience a real Sunday morning with Mac in her bed.

Since their time at the resort, they'd spent nearly every free moment together—in bed. They were like a couple of teenagers, determined to explore everything that sex had to offer, as quickly as possible.

"The drawings are really amazing," Mac murmured as he slowly paged through the book he'd picked up from her night table. "Look at the detail."

Emma curled her naked body against his, wrapping her arm around his waist. "We've done that one," she said.

"What do you think that box is for?" Mac asked. "What's inside?"

Emma had brought the *Kama Sutra* home a few weeks before and tossed it on the pile of books next to her bed. Mac had discovered it and now they were lazily paging through it in between bites of muffin and sips of coffee. "This one is interesting," she said.

"Do your legs bend like that?" he asked.

Emma frowned. "I'm not sure. Probably."

Mac chuckled. "I think we need to eliminate anything that might result in injury."

She sighed softly, her fingers distractedly twisting the hair on his lower abdomen. "How long are we going to keep this up?"

"Until we've tried everything in the *Kama Sutra*?" Mac said.

"I heard that Buddy is back. When were you going to tell me?"

Mac cursed, though he should have realized she'd find out. There was nothing that went unnoticed in this town, including Buddy's return from rehab.

"He came in yesterday," Mac said. "He's still not cleared to fly, but he's got a review set up for the end of the week."

"What happens if he's cleared?" Emma asked.

"He gets to fly again. But the way he's getting around, I doubt they'll clear him. He can't get in and out of the plane."

Emma shook her head. "You know what I mean. What happens with you…when he doesn't need you to fly anymore?"

"I guess I'm out of a job," Mac said.

Emma felt a surge of emotion, but she couldn't identify it. Was it sorrow? Regret? Was she angry that he was treating his leaving in such a glib manner? "Where will you go?"

He closed the book and set it on the night stand. "I've never really planned for the future. I've just gone where the wind blows me."

"Will you say goodbye before you let the wind blow you away from here?" Emma asked.

"Of course I will."

Emma wanted to ask him to stay. But she couldn't come up with a legitimate reason beyond the continuation of her sexual education. Was she falling in love with him? Of course she was. But any former virgin would have done the same. He was like her white knight, rescuing her from her lonely, sexless life. But Emma wasn't sure there was anything to it beyond that.

Mac had just said he wasn't the type to settle down, to find a regular job and buy a house or sign a lease. She had no idea what he thought about marriage and children. He owned a plane and some clothes and that had always been enough for him. He'd drifted for so long, could he ever adjust to a normal life? Could she? She'd been so focused on losing her virginity she hadn't given much thought to what came after.

She rolled on top of him, straddling his hips. "I'm glad you were the one," Emma said, smoothing her hands over his naked chest. "And no matter what happens, I'm never going to regret it."

"What do you think will happen?" Mac asked.

"I think someday, in the near future, you'll get in your plane and fly away and I'll never see you again." She pressed a kiss to the center of his chest. "Have you ever considered settling down? Getting married, maybe having a family?"

Mac shook his head. "I suppose I should want that. Most guys do. I've just always assumed that was something that wouldn't work for me. What about you?"

She laughed. "It's kind of hard to dream about marriage and family when you still haven't had sex. I guess I had other dreams that came first."

"What kind of dreams?"

"Traveling. Seeing the world."

"You're not afraid of flying anymore," he said. "And I'm not afraid of motel rooms anymore."

"What? You had a fear of motel rooms?"

"I can't—or couldn't fall sleep. I mean, anywhere else and I'm out in a few seconds. But a hotel or motel room? No sleep."

"You slept like a rock at the resort," she said. "You were even snoring."

"Yeah," he said. "I guess I finally put a pin in that particular fear. Or maybe you just tired me out."

"We were pretty…active," she said.

He reached up and smoothed the hair out of her eyes. "How are you going to feel when I leave?"

Emma drew a ragged breath and forced a smile. "Of course I'm going to be sad. But I'm going to try to prepare myself for that moment. And to appreciate that just because it ended, doesn't mean it wasn't wonderful while it was going on."

He slipped his hand around her neck and pulled her down into a long, sweet kiss. "I don't want to disappoint you," he murmured.

Emma snuggled closer. "How many women have you slept with?"

Mac gasped, drawing away from her to meet her gaze. "Are we really going to have this talk?"

She gathered her resolve. Emma had tried to be honest with him and wanted the same in return. And she'd always had a hard time containing her curiosity. "Yes," she said. "You know my number. What's yours?"

"I've honestly never counted," he said. "But it's probably less than you think."

She regarded him shrewdly. Was he going to make her guess? "What do you think I think?"

"I don't know. A couple hundred?"

The number was like a slap to the face. "No!" Emma said. "Two hundred? That's a lot of women. I mean, if you started at age—when did you start?"

"I was fifteen," he said. "I realize that's young, but I grew up fast. And she was older."

"And you're twenty-eight or twenty-nine now?"

"Twenty-seven," he said.

"So, twelve years. Two hundred women would be twelve or thirteen a year. Once a month?"

"There may have been a few years in my early twenties when I hit that number, but I can safely say it's probably more like sixty or seventy."

"The number doesn't really matter," Emma said.

"Thank you. I don't think it does, either."

She rested her chin on his chest. "Do you still talk to any of these women? Are you still friends? Or are they just…forgotten?"

"Are you asking if I'm going to forget you?"

Emma nodded. It was a silly request, she knew. But it was important to her. She wanted what they'd shared to matter. It didn't have to mean that they'd loved each other, but she wanted it to mean something.

"No, I won't forget you, Emma. Ever. I promise."

Relief flooded through her and she smiled. "Good. That makes me happy."

"I always aim to please," he said, reaching out to cup her cheek in his palm.

"We have to stop this now," she said, "or I'm never going to be able to let you go."

The ache began the moment she made the request. It was as if a part of her heart had been stolen, leaving an empty hole that physically hurt. Emma had known it was going to be difficult to let him go, but she hadn't expected it to hurt.

"So we're not going to see each other at all?" Mac asked.

"We'll see each other around town. Maybe at the library. We don't have to deliberately avoid each other, but we can't jump into bed every time we feel the urge."

He seemed reluctant to agree, but then he nodded. "You're right. It'll only make it more difficult in the end." He paused. "Do you want me to leave now?"

Emma ought to send him away. But that would take more courage than she could gather at such short notice. Instead, she'd be selfish and enjoy the rest of the day.

"No, stay. I'm going to make us some breakfast," she said. "What would you like? Pancakes or French toast? Or I can make eggs."

"You've never made French toast for me. I'll have that. Do you want me to help?"

Emma pulled on her robe, shaking her head. "Nope. You stay here and continue your research," she said, pointing to the *Kama Sutra*.

She hurried to the kitchen and began to pull out the ingredients for French toast. But she hesitated when she came to the syrup. Emma had always preferred cinnamon sugar on her French toast. What did Mac prefer? She had no idea.

Out of nowhere, tears pressed at the corners of her eyes. There were so many things she didn't know about him—simple, wonderful things that a lover deserved to know. But she wouldn't have the chance to find out.

She'd be left regretting that they'd never really known each other at all.

MAC ACCELERATED DOWN the runway, the fat tires of the Beaver bouncing along until the plane finally lifted off. He banked right and circled back around the hangar, then headed west toward Sonoma.

Drawing a deep breath of the fresh air, Mac smiled to himself. There wasn't a place he liked much better than a warm afternoon sky. Maybe a fancy resort shower with a naked woman in it? But the sky was much less complicated.

Since he'd taken up commercial flying five years ago, he'd never wanted to settle down in one spot. His nomadic and sparse life had fit him well. He'd never wanted more, and even if he had, he'd need an education. Hell, he'd barely graduated from high school and college had been out of the question. At eighteen, he'd been tossed out into the world to fend for himself.

Mac couldn't help but wonder what his life would have been like if his parents had never abandoned him in that motel room. Or if he'd had different parents. Would he be a doctor or a lawyer? Would he be living in some suburb with a pretty wife and a few children?

There were so many questions that needed answering, questions he'd avoided asking. Why? Would the answers make a difference? Mac knew exactly who and what he was and not many men could claim that. He'd made his choices in life and he was happy to live with them.

But this wasn't just about him anymore. He could see how Emma was struggling against everything she'd known in her life. She deserved more than just a series of wild nights in bed and a man willing to walk away. In another world, he could have been that man.

What would it feel like to have a woman truly care for him? To come home to her each night, to start a family?

He pulled back on the plane's yoke and climbed into the brilliant blue sky.

There were days when he'd wanted a dog or a comfortable sofa of his own. A pickup truck that didn't look as if it had been through a war. Maybe a few pictures on the wall and a big-screen television.

But Mac had learned that it didn't pay to want things. It only led to unhappiness and unreasonable expectations. Better to be satisfied with whatever came along down the road. He'd taught himself that early in life. The less he expected, the happier he would be.

But was he cheating himself out of a happy life? Maybe there wasn't anything wrong with wanting good things in your life. Wasn't that what living was all about? Mac groaned softly. Man, he was so screwed up. It would be a wonder if any woman would *want* to keep him around full-time.

Mac made a quick course correction, then shifted in his seat, his mind wandering back to the life he'd never had. What would he want or need to make a real life for himself? How much would it take? It usually came down to money. He'd always been content with what he made. But what if he put 100 percent effort into a career? Where would that land him?

The problem was, Mac wasn't qualified to do much more than fly a plane. He was a decent mechanic but that didn't pay much more than piloting did. If he wanted to provide a living for a wife and family, he needed something much bigger.

A few years ago, he'd flown organically grown herbs and lettuces to a produce market in San Francisco. Twice a week, he'd pack his plane and head north, dropping the boxes at a small airstrip south of the city. He'd seen the profit in that type of farming and had done some serious work in exploring the options.

But then another job came along and he let the dream drift away. Maybe it was time to take it out again and dust it off. If he made a profession for himself, then he'd have something to offer Emma—he'd have a future.

There was another element he needed to address. His past. He'd sent the DNA test in and then put it out of his mind. But now, he had to wonder whether there would be clues waiting there.

Mac knew that his lack of a family story bothered Emma. She couldn't seem to help herself, since she was a naturally curious person. There wasn't a question she couldn't answer with the combined forces of her library and the internet. Except the question of his past.

He'd never made a serious attempt to find out more about his family. Whenever he'd considered it, he'd backed away in fear of what he might find. But what if, after all this time, there was nothing bad to find? What if his mother regretted leaving him? What if they'd come back for him, only to find him gone, swept up in the foster care system?

The test had been so simple. A cotton swab wiped along the inside of the cheek, then popped into a plastic test tube. Mac had followed the directions and then put the tube into the prepaid envelope. The notion that he could have brothers and sisters, nieces and nephews…an entire family he never knew about… Mac chuckled to himself. After all this time, something so simple could change his life.

And yet, just because he wanted it, didn't mean it would happen. He could make the best life for himself, establish a career, find his family. But what if his family rejected him? What if the woman he loved couldn't stand the idea of living with him year after year? Not long after they'd made love, Emma had wanted to cool things off. And it hadn't seemed to affect her at all. Was he so easily cast aside?

Mac pushed his thoughts aside and made a quick scan of his gauges. The oil pressure was low and dropping. His attention shifted to the oil temperature gauge and noted it rising. He cursed softly and grabbed his radio.

"Stockton tower, this is November-seven-niner-two on a heading zero-two-zero out of San Coronado. I'm approximately twenty nautical miles from Stockton. I'm losing oil pressure."

"This is Stockton air traffic control. Are you declaring an emergency?"

"I'm going make a precautionary landing on an irrigation road in front of me," Mac said.

A loud bang shook the fuselage and dark smoke curled from the engine. He cursed softly. "Stockton tower, I am declaring an emergency. Look for me on the heading zero-two-zero." He paused. "And tell Emma that I love her."

Mac had handled a couple different midflight emergencies and come out unscathed, but this felt different. Smoke was beginning to seep into the cabin, making breathing difficult. There was real fear coursing through him and he found it difficult to accept his situation in a calm and rational manner. Damn it, he'd finally started to figure his life out and now it was going to end?

"Just work the problem," he murmured. Smoke burned his eyes and throat but he resisted opening the vents, knowing that would only add more oxygen to a fire. He went through his emergency procedures, fuel-off, altitude check, airspeed check, landing configuration. Squinting through the smoke he saw the irrigation road directly ahead.

Mac watched his air speed carefully as he went through his landing checklist—flaps, fuel, airspeed, gear. He had enough altitude to get there, but the sooner he put it on the ground, the higher his odds of getting out alive.

Mac put everything else out of his mind and focused on the plane. Thinking about the regrets in his life wouldn't increase his odds of survival.

When the wheels finally touched down on the rocky

dirt of an irrigation road, Mac let out a tightly held breath and laughed.

Mac pulled the plane to a stop and quickly shut down the engine. He threw open the door and as the smoke cleared from the cockpit he reached for the radio. "Stockton tower, this is November seven-niner-two. I'm on the ground and safe. No need for rescue. I should be able to get myself out of here."

Mac jumped out the open door, then bent down and kissed the ground. He ran his hands through his hair and drew a deep breath, before pulling his cell phone from his pocket. Better to keep all the drama between him and J.J. Emma didn't need to know the details of his trip. There were other things he intended to say to her.

There were no guarantees in life. Today proved that. And though Emma might reject him, he needed to hear her voice, to tell her how he felt before it was too late. He wanted so much more from her, hell, he deserved more. And now that he'd been given another chance, he was going to go after what he really wanted. No matter what it took.

THE EXPRESS ENVELOPE was propped up beneath the mailbox on Emma's front porch. She picked it up and scanned the return address, not recognizing the sender. Wandering over to one of the wicker chairs, she sank down into the chintz cushions and pulled the tab string, ripping open the top edge.

As she flipped though the sheaf of papers, Emma slowly realized what she was looking at. This was the DNA report on Mac. With a soft curse, she straightened the papers and shoved them back into the envelope, then set the envelope on the table beside her.

Emma pulled her cell phone from her purse and quickly dialed Trisha. When she heard her friend's voice on the other end of the phone, she quickly spoke. "I need you to come over right now. Are you finished with school? Can you come? It's an emergency."

"I'll be there in a few minutes," Trisha said.

Emma switched off the phone, then put some distance between her and the envelope. She sat down on the front porch steps, fighting the urge to grab the report and read it. She'd always been too curious for her own good, but reading that report before Mac did was just the wrong thing to do.

Since she'd ordered the kit and prepaid for the test, of course they'd send her the report. Maybe, if she called, they'd send another copy directly to Mac. Then he'd never have to know that she opened this one...and possibly read it, too.

"It was an innocent mistake," she said. But it wouldn't be innocent if she gave in to her curiosity and read the report. It was only natural that she'd want to learn the results. How could she be punished for surrendering to her natural instincts?

She folded her hands on her lap and tried to come up with a few more rationalizations, wondering how they might work on Mac. Several minutes later, Trisha's car screeched to a stop in front of the house. She hopped out and ran up the sidewalk.

"What is it? Are you all right? Are you pregnant? Are you gay? Are you dying?"

"No! Why would you ask those things?"

"You sounded so down on the phone. It was all I could think about on the ride over here."

"You thought I was gay?"

Trisha shrugged. "Up until a few days ago, you'd never had sex with a man. I wondered if you might have had a reason."

"I'm not gay. Not that I haven't wondered that myself. Nor am I sick or pregnant." She paused. "Well, I suppose I could be pregnant and just not know. I could be dying and not know, too. I could have a tumor."

"Stop!" Trisha cried, holding out her hands. "Let's start all over. Emma, you sounded upset on the phone. What's wrong? Please tell me."

Emma pointed over her shoulder. "It's that."

"The chair?"

"No, the envelope. On the table."

Trisha walked over to retrieve the envelope. "What is this?"

"It's the DNA report on Mac." She'd told Trisha all about Mac's lack of a past and the test that might help him find his family. So her best friend had all the information necessary to help her make the right judgment call on this issue. Emma could predict what she'd say—that this was private information and it was none of Emma's business. Emma just needed to hear the words out loud.

"Why do you have it?"

"I paid for the test when I sent for the kit," she said.

"How do you think Mac is going to react?"

"He said he doesn't want to know. I wouldn't be surprised if he threw it away. He doesn't want to live in the past."

"So this is more important to you than it is to him?"

Emma glanced over at her friend. "Yes?"

"Why?"

"Because I don't want him to be alone in the world. I don't like to think that when he leaves here—when he leaves me—that he'll be alone."

"What if he doesn't leave? What if he stays?"

Emma shook her head. "He wouldn't stay. There's nothing here for him."

"There's you," Trisha said. "You can say it out loud, Em. You want him to stay. You want to make a life with him. But in order for that to be possible, you have to find out the truth about his background, just to make sure."

"I don't," Emma said. "To all of that. He can't stay. And he's not the kind of guy who settles down. And I shouldn't care what that report says."

"If that's all true, then go ahead and read it," Trisha said. "You have nothing to lose."

"No," Emma said. "I'm not going to read it. I'm going to give it to him."

"What if he doesn't want to open it? What if he throws it away?"

Emma frowned. "I wasn't joking about that. It's a real possibility. He's weird about his past." She groaned, covering her face with her hands. "I'm just going to scan it quickly. There's probably nothing to there anyway. What are the chances that they'd find any relatives?"

"Pretty slim," Trisha said.

"All right," Emma said, holding out her hand. "Just a quick peek." Trish handed her the envelope and Emma withdrew the papers again. Drawing a deep breath, she flipped through the pages. "Here it is," she said. "Number of matches." Her breath caught in her throat, and for a long time, Emma didn't breathe. Finally, she gasped. "Twenty-six. Oh, my God, he has twenty-six people who are a genetic match to him in this database."

"But they could be distant cousins," Trisha said. "Tenth or eleventh cousins, twice removed."

"No, no, it says here that Mac shares a great-grandfather with this one. And a great-great-grandfather with this one." She turned to the next page and stopped. "Oh." Tears suddenly flooded her eyes and she pressed her hand to her chest, trying to swallow down the flood of emotion.

"What is it?" Trisha asked.

Emma held the papers out to Trisha and she took them. "Q-1087. Relationship, brother. Q-1088. Relationship, mother. Oh, my God, Emma. You found his family."

"I found their DNA."

"I don't understand," Trisha said.

"This database was originally set up for genealogists. It—it was designed to help them find connections. If you know you have a genealogical connection to someone, you can trace that connection back and figure out how you're related."

"I still don't get it. Why would all these people put their DNA on the site?"

"Some people use the site to find lost relatives or birth parents. It looks like this group is searching for people in their family."

"These all have an asterisk. What does that mean?"

Emma looked over Trisha's shoulder. "Here," she said, pointing to a footnote. "Quinn Family Search. Contact ASAP. The *Q* beside the numbers must stand for Quinn."

The name pricked at Emma's mind. Quinn. She'd read something in one of her journals recently. Quinn. Aileen Quinn. She was one of Emma's favorite authors, famous in her native Ireland. Suddenly, Emma jumped to her feet. "Wait here," she said.

She ran into the house and hurried down the long hallway to her mother's old office. There was a stack of professional journals on the corner of the desk and she picked through the magazines, searching for the right issue. It had to be here, she thought. She never threw away one of her journals.

"Em?" Trisha's voice echoed through the screen door. "Em, do you want help in there?"

"Hang on," Emma shouted. "I just need to find this…one…thing. I'm sure it's here."

After a five-minute search, she found the right edition on the bottom of the stack she'd set on the floor.

"Aileen Quinn," she read, sitting back on her heels. "The Search for Family."

Emma hurried back to the porch and sat down beside Trisha. "This is a story about the author Aileen Quinn. She grew up believing she was an orphan, but when she started researching her autobiography, she learned that she had four older brothers who were sent away when she was just a baby. She's been searching for their descendants for the past three or four years." She took a deep breath and let it out slowly. "I think the *Qs* in this report might be the descendants she found."

"And the family put their DNA into this database because they're still looking for someone," Trisha said.

"They're looking for Mac," Emma said. "And when they find him, Aileen Quinn is going to give him a huge inheritance. His whole life will change."

A long silence grew between them. Finally Trisha spoke. "You need to tell him," she murmured. "Right away. You can't keep this from him."

Emma groaned, leaning back and closing her eyes. "I know. And I'll also have to tell him that I read the whole report. Or maybe I should just leave the envelope and the journal at his door and run away."

"You're the one who started this, Em. You're going to have to follow through."

Emma slowly stood, clutching the evidence to her chest. "All right. I'm going to go find him and tell him who he is. And I'm going to pray that he considers this happy news and doesn't kill the messenger."

Trisha laughed. "Do you want me to come with you?"

She shook her head. "Nope. I can handle it." Emma went inside and grabbed her car keys and purse and ran a brush through her hair.

She and Mac had cleverly avoided any talk of a future between them. Since she'd rid herself of her virginity, she had enjoyed all the pleasures of no-strings sex and she suspected that Mac was quite happy with their arrangement.

But it was time to get back to real life, to recognize that they were completely unsuited for each other. But would this news she had for him be too "real" for Mac's life? Would she ruin the delicate balance that he'd achieved living entirely in the present? The only way to find out was to give him the package. And if he hated her afterward, she'd accept that as punishment for her meddling.

But as she drove out to the airstrip, Emma was faced with the stark realization that she didn't want to risk his anger. Because she was in love with Luke MacKenzie, or whatever his real name turned out to be. And this news might just be what sent him running.

7

BUDDY, J.J. AND Mac sat on a row of crates just inside the huge hangar door. They sipped cold beers, served in longneck bottles, as they stared out into the midafternoon sunshine.

"Where are you headed next?" Buddy asked.

Mac took a long sip of his beer. "I haven't decided. I thought I'd stick around here for another week while I line up some jobs."

"You're welcome to stay," Buddy said. "You've done a good job with the crop dusting. And it's going to be a while before I can fly a plane myself. Got to stop taking the pain medication first."

"How are you feeling?" Mac asked.

"Old," Buddy said. "Way too old." He shook his head. "Where did all the years go?"

"You have regrets?" Mac asked.

"Sure, I got plenty," Buddy said. "I never settled down, found myself a wife. I always figured I'd have time for all that. Then suddenly I didn't. I would have liked to have kids. Maybe done a bit more traveling.

Now I got these bum hips, I can't barely make it from one side of the hangar to the other. You boys take some advice from me. It's no treat to be alone. Find yourselves a nice woman."

J.J. leaned forward and fixed his gaze on something outside the hangar. "Speaking of women, is that Emma Bryant tearing up the road there?"

Mac squinted against the sunlight, surprised when he recognized the battered Volvo. "Yep, that's her. I wonder what she's coming out here for."

"I thought it was over between you two," J.J. said.

"I told you that was only temporary," Mac said, pushing to his feet.

He'd definitely missed her. His nights hadn't been the same, sleeping on the lumpy cot at the hangar, no soft, sweet body to touch, no smiles when he woke up in the morning. He was still as determined to explore what was between him and Emma as he'd been in that field after his near-accident. He just hadn't figured out how to put it to her.

But, hell, Buddy was right. If he wanted that for the rest of his years, a woman in his bed and in his life, then he'd damn well have to do something about it.

Emma pulled the car up in front of the hangar door and got out. J.J. and Buddy watched her, and Mac heard Buddy say to J.J., "If I were thirty years younger, there's the girl I'd take a chance on. She's pretty, she's smart and she can bake a helluva cake."

Mac walked up to the driver's-side window of her car and leaned in. "Hi. What are you doing out this way?"

"We need to talk," Emma said. "Do you have some time?"

"Sure," he said. "You want to stay here or go somewhere else?"

"Get in," she said.

Mac circled the car and slipped into the passenger seat. Emma made a wide U-turn and headed back down the road. "We'll get ice cream," she said, glancing his way. "Everything goes better with ice cream. Have you been to the Dairy Bar?"

Mac shook his head. "Never been."

"You'll like it. They make a cherry chocolate chip with fresh cherries that's really—"

"What is this all about, Em? You seem flustered."

"I'll tell you when we have ice cream," she said.

"So it's bad?"

"No, it's great. Really. At least part of it is."

Mac managed to contain his curiosity for the rest of the trip to the ice cream stand. As Emma had promised, the stand featured three different ice cream specials, including the cherry chocolate chip. She ordered a single scoop in a bowl and he ordered two scoops. They found a table in a small grassy area next to the parking lot.

She set a large envelope on the table in front of her. "These are the results of your DNA test. You'll notice that the envelope is open, so let me explain that first. I didn't recognize the sender on the envelope, so I opened it and then realized that it was the report on your test."

"Did you read it?" he asked.

"Not at first," she said. "But then I was concerned

that you might throw it away and no one would know and I convinced myself I was doing a good thing and—" She drew a ragged breath. "I'm sorry. I shouldn't have been nosy and you have every right to be angry with me and—"

"What did it say?"

Now that the results were in front of him, Mac wasn't sure he wanted to read them. Considering the look on her face, the odds were probably against a happy ending. If no matches had been found, then he'd be left with the realization that he would always be alone in the world. If there was a match somewhere out there, he'd face the choice of chasing it down or letting it go.

"I should have never agreed to this," he murmured. "My life was fine the way it was. I was happy. I didn't have any questions about my past. I didn't care. And now, you set this…Pandora's box in front of me and expect me to open it."

"I've already opened it," Emma said.

"So I let you judge whether it's good or bad?"

"What if it gives you a name? An identity?" She paused. "A brother."

Mac met her gaze, searching her face for the truth in her words. A brother? How could that be? Why would his parents leave him behind only to have another child? They could have come back to get him but instead, they'd chosen to start a family all over again.

He pushed the envelope away. "Burn it," he said. "I don't want to know more. And I don't care what you think."

Mac pushed up from the table and strode toward

the street. He wasn't sure where he was going, but he needed to get away from that envelope. Emma followed after him, calling his name. But he refused to slow his pace, his anger fueling his energy.

"Mac, wait! There's more. It's not all bad, I promise."

He spun around and held out his hand, warning her off. "Emma, let it go. I don't want to see it."

She approached him slowly and when she got close enough, she reached out and smoothed her hand across his cheek. "All right. I understand. But I'm not going to burn it. Someday, you might want to read that report."

"This is important to you, isn't it?" he said, his gaze fixed on hers. "You need this more than I do."

"Maybe I do," Emma admitted. "Maybe I believe that if you finally knew who you were, you'd quit trying to run away from life."

"I'm not running away from life, I'm living it," he said. "I'm just not living *your* life. Why the hell would I want to stay stuck in some small fishbowl town like this, where everyone's got their nose in your business? Why would I want to be with the same woman for the rest of my life? Be burdened with a family and job that I hated, only to be traded in for a better man, a more reliable worker somewhere down the line."

The words seemed to tumble out of his mouth without any filter or restraint. As he was shouting at her, Mac knew he didn't mean most of what he was saying. Since he'd met Emma, he'd wanted a life with all the traditional trappings. He was tired of running from the past.

But what if he couldn't be what Emma wanted or

deserved? What if he failed at the one thing in life he truly wanted? He had to offer her something beyond great sex. If he didn't, she'd grow tired of him and start looking for what she really needed—security, a man who could provide for her.

Every instinct inside him told him to run away. But if he did, he'd leave behind any chance he had for a life with Emma.

"I have to go," he said. He leaned forward and brushed a kiss across her lips. "Thank you for doing this for me."

She held up the envelope. "You don't want it?"

He shook his head. "You keep it. I'll talk to you later."

"Let me take you back to Buddy's," she said.

"No, I need to walk."

"I'm so sorry. I should have never forced you to do this."

He kissed her again, this time lingering over her mouth for a long while. "No, you were right. And you're not to blame, Em. My scars run really deep, and as you can see, it doesn't take a whole lot to expose them. I don't remember much of my past, but I know that it wasn't happy. And if I allow myself to dwell on that, I'm afraid that my present life will feel like...like a fraud." He gave her hand a squeeze. "Don't worry. I'm fine."

With that Mac spun on his heel and walked away. He fought the instinct to turn around and look at her once more. Was this the last time he'd speak to her? He had to leave, yet he couldn't make himself get in his plane and go.

How could he ever forget her? She'd managed to crawl inside him and carve out a little place in his heart, a spot that would always seem empty without her. Mac had tried to understand his feelings for her, but the only explanation he could come up with was that he was in love with Emma.

This had all seemed pretty simple at the start, Mac mused. A sexual attraction, the possibility of a short but sweet affair. And now, he realized that he'd fallen into quicksand. There was no good way to get out, at least not without hurting Emma.

Love. It was a word that he'd never thought he'd use in relation to a woman. In truth, he'd never believed himself capable of falling in love. But this feeling defied explanation, and he was beginning to doubt that he'd ever find real happiness without her.

Why did life have to be so damn complicated?

"IMAGINE THE worst way it could have gone and then triple it," Emma said. "That's how it went. I didn't even get a chance to tell him about the money. He cut me off long before that. When he found out he had a brother."

Trisha drew her inside her apartment and closed the door behind Emma. "Was he angry? Or hurt?"

"Both. I went in there thinking how wonderful the news would be. He had a brother. It never occurred to me that he'd assume his parents had abandoned him just so they could replace him with another son. Can you imagine how that would hurt?"

"Was he angry at you?"

"No, not at me. He kissed me. Several times, so I'm

pretty sure he wasn't upset that I read the contents of the envelope."

"Well, that's something," she said in an encouraging tone. "That's what you were worried about."

"Yes, but I didn't get to tell him everything. He could very well inherit a million dollars. Who wouldn't be happy about a million-dollar windfall? I should have just blurted that out and taken my chances with the rest. It might have soothed some of the pain about his brother."

Trisha sat silently for a long moment, her brow furrowed.

"What?" Emma asked. "Say what you're thinking."

"Do you still have the report?" Trisha asked.

"No, I gave it to Mac."

"I'm just trying to remember that entry for his brother. The birth year. Wasn't it two years before Mac's?"

"Yes, you're right," Emma said. She gasped softly. "If he had a brother two years older than him, Mac should have known him. I don't get it. How is that possible? His mother was listed as well, so—"

"We're looking at this the wrong way," Trisha said. "We're assuming that the people that Mac remembers as his parents are his birth parents. What if they aren't?"

Emma leaped up from the sofa. "I posed that question to him myself, but he never really considered the possibility. It would explain a lot of things, and now we have more evidence that points to it." She felt a flood of emotion. "What if he's already left?"

"You just saw him."

"He has a plane. He can just hop on board and fly away at a moment's notice."

"Where did you leave things?"

Emma shrugged. "He just walked away." She felt tears burning at the corners of her eyes. She didn't want to cry. She'd worked so hard not to care about him, and now, like every other silly single woman, she'd let a man steal her heart.

"You're in love with him, aren't you?" Trisha said.

Emma nodded. "Of course I am. I was so stupid to think that I could keep this all about the sex." She shook her head. "I feel so ridiculous."

"No, no," Trisha said, wrapping her arm around Emma's shoulders. "You're in love. That's a wonderful thing, Em. Now you know that it's possible. And the next man you meet, you'll have a wonderful romance and a fabulous sex life."

"I liked the sex I had with Mac," she said, wiping at her runny eyes.

Trisha got up and fetched a wad of paper towel from the kitchen, then handed it to Emma. "Have you told him that you love him?"

"No!" Emma cried. "I can't do that. We had an agreement. I promised I wasn't going to develop any feelings for him."

"But you have! Surprise, surprise. You met a handsome, funny and clever man. He took you to bed and you fell in love with him." Trisha's eyes went wide and she clapped her hands to her cheeks. "I don't think that's ever happened before in the entire history of the world!"

Emma laughed through her tears. "I don't sound nearly as pathetic when you put it that way."

"See, the situation seems better already. And now, you're going to find your man and you're going to tell him exactly how you feel. And if he still takes off into the sunset, then he wasn't the man you thought he was."

"You're right." She'd get in her car and she'd drive around town until she found him.

She gave Trisha a hug. "At least my life is exciting now," Emma said with a giggle.

Her car was waiting where she parked it and Emma got inside and turned the ignition.

She would be honest with Mac about how much he meant to her and deal with the consequences. They weren't a couple of kids, playing at love and sex. They were adults who were fully capable of making sensible decisions about their feelings for each other.

Emma pulled up in front of her house and hopped out of the car. But she slowed her step when she saw Mac slouched in one of the wicker chairs on the porch, his long legs stretched out in front of him. He stood as she approached.

Emma's heart slammed into her chest and she racked her mind for something to say. She'd decided to tell him exactly what was in her heart, but now that he was here, in person, she couldn't seem to form an intelligent sentence.

He slowly descended the front steps and in a few long strides he was in front of her, sweeping her up into his arms and kissing her deeply.

There wasn't any need to speak, Emma thought. His kiss revealed everything she needed to know. He yearned for her, he wanted her, he forgave her. Her fingers tangled in the hair at his nape and she moaned softly as his tongue explored the inner recesses of her mouth.

She'd come to love the taste of him, the scent that clung to his body after a shower, the warmth that seeped through her clothes when he held her. Every time she touched him, Emma discovered something new and exciting. There were a lifetime of discoveries hidden in his body and his mind.

Mac scooped her up into his arms and carried her inside the house, setting her back onto her feet once he'd shut the door. His fingers moved to the buttons on her blouse and he quickly worked through them before pushing her cardigan and blouse off her shoulders.

He seemed almost frantic to undress her. Emma helped him along until she stood in front of him, completely naked. She watched as his gaze skimmed the length of her body, followed by the touch of his fingers. A shiver skittered over her body and her breath caught in her throat as he teased at her nipple.

They'd had many intimate encounters since that first one, and they'd all been crazy and exciting and filled with passion. But this would be different. She loved him, and as his hands caressed her body, she repeated the sentiment over and over in her mind. If she were brave and confident, she might have had the courage to say it out loud. But for now, it was enough to acknowledge it in her heart.

Emma slowly circled him, then reached around his torso to grab the lapels of his canvas jacket. She drew it down over his broad shoulders, then tossed it aside.

Piece by piece, she removed his clothes and when he was naked, she stood in front of him and smiled.

"Now what am I going to do with you?" she murmured.

"Whatever you want to do," he said with a lazy smile.

"I thought we both agreed that it would be better if this didn't happen again."

"We did," he replied. "I have no idea how I lost my clothes. Do you remember how you lost yours?"

Emma smiled, shaking her head. "Maybe we were wrong?"

He wrapped his arm around her waist and pulled her close, then slipped his fingers between her legs. Slowly, he began to caress her, his fingers slick with her desire. "Anything that feels this good can't be all bad, can it?"

Emma's knees weakened and she leaned against him for balance. She loved the way he took possession of her body, the way he knew exactly what would make her tremble with pleasure. Every time they were together, it just got better and better.

Her reply to his question didn't come in words, but in action. She reached down and gently wrapped her fingers around his hard shaft, stroking it from base to tip. A soft moan slipped from his throat and he bent close to kiss her.

This is how it always begins, she mused. Slow and deliberate. And then, the need would become too much and desperation would set in. They'd be frantic for that moment when he would plunge inside her, and then they'd fixate on reaching their release together.

Just thinking about what was to come was enough to send a shiver through her body. His fingers continued to tease her, coaxing her closer to the edge.

Was this how it would always be between them? she wondered. Or would the passion cool and the need finally subside? Emma had no benchmarks, no previous men to compare him to. But she couldn't imagine ever wanting a man more than she wanted Mac.

"Take me to the bedroom," Emma whispered, fighting the urge to surrender to him then and there.

He didn't answer her. Instead, he increased his rhythm until her resolve crumbled in a wild storm of pleasure and torment. She whispered his name as the spasms rocked her.

This was exactly where she belonged. Forever.

MAC STRETCHED OUT on the soft bed, throwing his arm over his eyes to avoid his ongoing study of the ceiling of Emma's bedroom. He'd been living in San Coronado for over a month now and was still essentially homeless. It was a condition that had never really bothered him in the past. But since meeting Emma and beginning their odd little affair, he'd begun to look at things differently.

She'd made a place for herself in his life. In turn, he'd allowed her into his heart, and now, the choices he made were choices that the both of them had to live with.

Mac knew what the folks around town thought of him—he was a drifter, a guy without any goals or aspirations. And they might have been right a month ago.

But now that his life had shifted on its axis, Mac found himself planning for the future.

Though he didn't have a fancy diploma hanging on the wall, he was sure he could make more of himself than he already had. And he'd been mulling over an idea for the past week that promised to provide a regular income and a permanent home. He'd require financing, though. More money than could be provided by selling his plane and cashing in his savings. He'd need to find a banker who was willing to give him a loan.

Mac knew it would be twice as hard for him as it would be for most men. He didn't have a family to back him up, a father or grandfather with money to invest. He had no history, no credit cards, no résumé. Life had always been more complicated for people like him.

"People like me," he murmured. "What does that even mean?"

His thoughts wandered back to the envelope. He'd been so freaked out by the prospect of what might be inside that he really hadn't listened to what Emma had tried to say to him. Had there been nothing but bad news to report, she would have told him that straight off. But she hadn't. There was some hope inside that report.

Hope that he could finally have answers to the questions that had dogged him for years. What had happened to his parents? Did he have other relatives? If he was completely honest with himself, there wasn't much more he could learn that could hurt him. Hell, he'd been left behind in a seedy hotel room. How much worse could it get? If his parents had had another child, maybe they'd abandoned him, as well. If Mac found him, maybe they could learn to heal together.

Mac closed his eyes. It was partly his fault that his parents had abandoned him. In the months prior, his father had been trying to get Mac to learn the basics of grifting—how to cheat a cashier, how to pick a pocket, how to cheat at cards and dice. His mother had shown him how to act as a distraction when she shoplifted food or other necessities. But Mac had steadfastly refused to participate, unable to rationalize the crimes he'd known he'd been committing.

Somewhere, buried deep inside him, was a morality that he had inherited from someone. But if not from the people he assumed were his parents, then from whom?

Mac carefully slipped out of bed, leaving Emma curled up beneath the sheets and blankets, a naked leg the only skin exposed to the chill of the room.

He walked over to the window, drawing in the cold night air deeply. He closed the window, then found his jeans and tugged them on, zipping them up but leaving the button undone at the waist. He walked down the hall to the living room, slowly scanning the room.

He tried to recall what she'd done with the envelope after they'd left the ice cream stand. She'd had a bag over her arm when she'd sat down with the ice cream. But she hadn't had the bag when she'd come into the house earlier in the evening.

He walked through the house and out into the night, his bare feet silent on the brick front walk. As he suspected, the book bag was on the front seat of her car. He pulled it out and walked back inside the house.

Mac flipped on a light next to an overstuffed chair and sat down.

The envelope was inside the bag. He pulled the package out and removed the papers inside. Drawing a deep breath, he began to go through them, one by one. He didn't take time to read the explanations. He was too impatient to understand the results. Nothing made sense.

He found a copy of a library journal on the bottom of the pile, open to an article about a lady named Quinn. Cursing softly, Mac tossed that aside and went back to the report's tables and charts.

"What are you doing?"

Mac looked up to find Emma standing in the shadows near the hallway. She was wrapped up in the cotton blanket from the bed, her hair tumbling around her face.

"I'm trying to read this DNA report. But I don't understand it."

Emma came over and he pulled her down onto his lap. She took the papers from his hand and went through them until she found the page she was looking for. "You had multiple matches," she said.

"Multiple?"

Emma nodded. "See. They're all listed here by these numbers. Most of them are third cousins, which means you share a great-great-grandparent. And then there's this." She pointed to a spot on the page.

Mac turned the page toward the light. "Brother?"

"And mother," she said.

"My mother sent in her DNA? Why would she do that?"

"I don't think this mother in the report is the same woman who left you in the hotel room. This is your birth mother," Emma said, pointing to the page.

Mac stared at the paper for a long time, his expression unchanging. "How is it possible that I have a birth mother?"

"She could have put you up for adoption. You could have been kidnapped. There are all sorts of possibilities. And look. This brother is two years *older* than you. If those people you knew as your parents had given birth to him, wouldn't he have been with you?"

"I never had a brother. I would have remembered that." Mac leaned back into the soft chair, the news hitting him like a kick to the stomach. "Maybe there's been some kind of mistake," he said.

"Maybe. But these DNA people are probably pretty careful about their work." She paused. "There's something else. All these numbers are marked with a star, and if you go to this box, you'll see that means they are part of the Quinn Family Search. I remembered something I'd read in one of my library journals about Aileen Quinn, the famous Irish author. She's been searching for descendants of her four brothers and has been dividing her estate among the Quinns she finds. I think these people, all these *Q* numbers, are *her* Quinns. And you're one of them."

"Quinn. I don't recognize the name at all."

"And here it says your brother and mother are also Quinns. They'll probably know how you got separated from the rest of the family. That's if you want to know. You don't have to contact them if you don't want to.

Unless you give your permission, they have no way of tracing you."

"I'd be stupid if I didn't follow through on this," he said.

"There's also the million dollars," she said.

Mac frowned. "What?"

"That's the share of Aileen's estate that each descendant gets."

"Where does it say that?" he asked, rifling through the papers.

"In the article. There's a documentary about the search, too. I think you can stream it on FilmBuff." She pulled a sheet from the stack. "But first, if you really want to follow through on this, you have to start by opening an account with the DNA company so that others in the Quinn Family Search can contact you and you can contact them."

"How do we do that?"

"We call this phone number and punch in a code to unlock your account. And then we wait and see if your relatives contact us. Unless their code is open and then we can contact them."

"How long do you think it will take?"

"Not long," she said.

Mac wrapped his arms around her and gave her a fierce hug. "This could completely change my life. I might have a brother and a mother."

"A mother who knows you're out there. They may be actively searching for you."

"I would probably be hard to find."

"There is another place we could look," Emma said. "If they are searching for you, then they've probably posted on some adoption sites. We have a name now and a birth year. And you have a brother. We could try to find out more."

Mac shook his head. "I've found out enough for tonight," he said. "I need time to adjust." He drew a deep breath. "Quinn. That's Irish, right?"

"I think so," Emma said.

"It's the first piece of information I've had about my family. But I'm afraid to believe it. It could be wrong."

"You'll know soon enough. Can you imagine getting that kind of money?"

Mac chuckled softly. "That's the one thing I'm not sure I'll ever let myself believe. Money like that just doesn't fall out of the sky."

Emma crawled out of his lap and held out her hand. "Come on, let's go back to bed. In the morning, we'll call and open the account."

He got to his feet and pulled Emma into his arms, nuzzling his face into her neck as he hugged her. "Thank you for this," Mac said. He could have gone the rest of his life never learning the truth, and because of Emma's natural curiosity, in the matter of a single night, he had a whole herd of relatives.

As he held her in his arms, Mac felt an overwhelming sense of contentment, something he'd never experienced in the past. Now was the time to tell her that he loved her. But there was still something holding him back.

He'd wait until he knew exactly who he was. And if he was going to inherit a million dollars from a lost aunt. If all that was true, then there was a chance he could build a comfortable life for them both.

But right now, all he could focus on was the next two hours in bed with Emma. They still had a few hours before he had to fly fresh microgreens and herbs to the farmers' market in San Francisco.

"Come on," he said, lacing his fingers through hers. "I need to get you out of that blanket and back into bed. You shouldn't be up this late."

Emma giggled, then tore the sheet off her naked body and threw it in his face. "I'll race you. First one there gets to pick the page out of the *Kama Sutra*."

She ran ahead of him and Mac groaned. Though he'd come to appreciate Emma's adventurous nature in the bedroom, he wanted to send the *Kama Sutra* back to the library. It brought more laughs then truly satisfying sex.

As he started down the hall, he realized it didn't matter. Their relationship didn't have a deadline anymore. It wasn't inevitable that he'd move on with his life in a different place, and once Emma knew that, surely she wouldn't want to break up. If everything turned out right, this could be his place, in this sweet little Victorian house in San Coronado with the town's sexy librarian.

8

"AS YOU CAN SEE, we've met all our goals, even with the reduction of funds from the county library budget," Emma said. "I think we'll be able to continue this level of service well into our next fiscal year without any major disruptions."

A polite round of applause broke out and Emma smiled in appreciation. Her monthly meeting with the library board was a major event on her calendar, and they'd had some meetings that had grown quite contentious. But things at the San Coronado Public Library had been humming along quite nicely lately.

Emma had managed to carry on with both her job and a love affair without having to compromise on either. And though she was unclear about the future with Mac, she'd decided that, like him, she'd live in the present and enjoy each day as it came.

"That's all for our agenda," Mrs. Belton said, "is there any other new business that we need to address?"

"I do have some new business," Mrs. Fincutter said, raising a trembling hand. "But I believe this is a subject that should be discussed in executive session, so I move that we adjourn the public portion of this meeting and move into executive session."

"Do I have a second on that motion?" Mrs. Belton asked.

The public meeting was concluded and the six members of the community who had attended filed out of the room, leaving Emma and the seven members of the board.

The library board had always been made up of some of the town's most powerful social leaders. Though they were a difficult group to please, Emma had managed to figure them all out and avoid any major battles. But oddly, she wasn't sure what this executive session was all about.

"Minerva, I'm going to ask that you stop taking notes, as this part of the meeting is going to be off the record."

"Can we do that?" Minerva Butterworth asked. "This is still an official meeting."

"All right, then, I move to adjourn the meeting, but I request that all members of the board remain in the room until dismissed."

"I don't know if that's legal, either," Louise Fincutter said.

"Well, I say it is," Madge Belton said, rapping her gavel on the table, "and if any of you have a problem with that, we can discuss it after this little social gathering disperses." She gave everyone in the room the eyeball and the other six women nodded in compliance.

"We have some concerns on a personal level that we'd like to discuss with you, Emma. Before they turn into something that the library board might have to act upon."

"Concerns? I don't understand."

"It's the man," Leonora Brady said, her voice cracking.

"The man?"

"The… I can't really call him a gentleman," Madge said.

"Stranger," Leonora said. "Call him a stranger."

"This stranger," Madge continued, "that you've been carrying on with."

"With *whom* you've been carrying on," Regina Farley corrected. She was a retired English teacher.

"We all have…concerns," Madge continued. "This man is entirely unsuitable for you. What do you know about him? He has no family, no connections. He just appeared out of nowhere and inserted himself into your life in a very unseemly manner."

Emma gasped. She couldn't believe what they were saying. Sure, they had always interfered in her personal life, trying to set her up on blind dates or suggest places where she might meet single men. But never had they directly questioned her personal choices or threatened her job.

She pushed to her feet and began to gather her things. "My relationship with Mac is really none of your business," she murmured. "And I won't stay here and listen to this."

"Sit down!" Madge ordered, her tone of voice stern.

Emma looked down at her but remained standing.

"You forget that all of us here were very dear friends of your mother's, God rest her soul. And we owe it to her to speak up. She would not approve of this behavior, Emma."

"What behavior?" Emma asked, tipping her chin up.

"I don't think we need to spell it out," Madge said. "You have always been a sterling example of propriety and good sense in this town. Children look up to you. Adults admire you."

"We really don't mean to interfere," Louise said.

"Oh, yes, we do," Leonora countered. "And personally, I believe what you're doing is wrong, Emma."

"Stop," Emma said. "You don't have to go on."

"Good," Madge said. "I'm glad you've seen the error of your ways. You've always been a sensible girl. Your mother would be proud."

"My mother would want me to be happy. And I *am* happy. I don't care if you approve of Luke MacKenzie. I'm the one who's sleeping with him, so my opinion is the only one that matters."

Madge gasped. "Then you won't break it off with him?"

"I know you've always hoped that your grandson, Charlie Clemmons, might capture my affections, but that's not going to happen, Madge."

"You're refusing to put this man out of your life?" Louise asked.

"I am," Emma said. "But I'll go one better for you. I'll put you and the ladies of the library board out of my life, along with the library itself. I resign my position effective immediately." Emma scooped up her files and her purse.

"There's no reason to be hasty," Madge said. "We certainly didn't expect a resignation."

Emma smiled. "Neither did I. But now that I have resigned, I think it's exactly what I needed to do. I've been hanging around this town for years, waiting for my life to happen, waiting for something or someone to come and shake things up. But these last few weeks with Mac, I've discovered that I'm perfectly capable of shaking things up all on my own. So it's time for me to step out of my comfort zone and see what's waiting out there for me. Ladies, thank you for the encouragement."

As she strode out of the room, she heard chaos break out among the ladies. Accusations flew, punctuated by the frantic rap of Madge's gavel. Emma didn't look back.

She didn't bother stopping in her office. There wasn't anything there that she wanted, and, in truth, she was desperate to take a deep breath of the outside air.

As she walked down the front steps of the library, Emma's legs became wobbly and she quickly sat down. She hadn't realized that her heart was slamming into her chest or that her pulse was racing. A strange buzz filled her head and when she took a deep breath, she felt a bit nauseous.

"What have I done?" she murmured.

The library was her life's work. She'd never even dreamed of leaving the job. But in that moment, when her morals were being questioned and Mac's motives maligned, it had all made sense. It was time to move on, time for her to make choices for herself and not for others.

She was frightened and exhilarated and giddy and

confused all at once. Exactly the way she'd felt when she'd first met Mac. But look at the changes he'd brought to her life. He'd given her the courage to break free, he'd shown her a way to live in the present and to stop worrying about the future or regretting the past.

Emma got to her feet and walked to her car. She got in and started it. Taking a deep breath, Emma placed her hands on the wheel.

This was good, she told herself. She had plenty of savings to tide her over until she figured out her next move. The house was paid for. Maybe she'd take a few months off and travel. Certainly there were more interesting places to live than San Coronado. Now that she'd nearly conquered her fear of flying, the world was open to her.

Or maybe she'd see what happened with Mac. If he had to go find his family— Emma stopped herself. Had she just made it possible for her to follow Mac wherever he happened to go?

"No, no, no," Emma said. That hadn't even come to mind. And yet, she couldn't deny that part of her wanted him to stay. And if he couldn't stay, then maybe, deep inside, she wanted to be free to leave with him.

This was not about Mac! This was about her taking control of her life and stepping out into the world. She wasn't the 27-year-old virgin anymore. She was a woman who knew exactly what she wanted from life.

Emma put the car in gear and pulled out of the library parking lot. She looked in the rearview mirror. That may have been the last time she'd step inside a building that had been a home to her for most of her life.

Her thoughts drifted to Mac. He'd lived his whole life in the present and now, because of her, he suddenly had a past—and a future. A million-dollar inheritance could buy him so many opportunities.

She wouldn't tell him what she'd done. In a few days, he'd hear from Aileen Quinn and he'd be off on a new adventure. There was no reason for him to know, especially if he might question her motives. She had no designs on a future with him and she had to find her own way now more than ever—and she needed to keep telling herself exactly that.

Emma steered the car to Trisha's apartment. Her friend would understand. And her winter break was coming up soon. Maybe they could find a nice tropical island to visit. Or maybe Paris, Emma thought. Christmas in Paris would be a dream come true.

Though the holiday season was typically a bit slow at the library, Emma had always volunteered to take as many shifts as she could, allowing her assistants to enjoy the time with their families. But now she was free to do as she pleased.

She brushed aside a flood of guilt. She wasn't going to regret what she'd done. It was over. From this moment on, her life would be completely different, and she had no intention of going back.

Emma grabbed her cell phone from her bag and hit Trisha's speed dial key. When her friend picked up, Emma drew a deep breath. "Crack open a bottle of wine. I'm on my way over and I have big news."

"How big?" Trisha asked.

"Enormous," Emma replied.

MAC PACED THE length of Emma's living room, then turned and started in the opposite direction. "Maybe I should have waited," he said. "Given myself a few more days to absorb this information."

Emma watched him from her spot on the arm of the easy chair. "You could call him and tell him you need more time. He left a cell phone number."

"Mobile," Mac said. "That's what he called it. His 'mobile,' with a long *I*."

"Mobile," she repeated. "So call his mobile and put it off."

"He's come all the way from Ireland. I can't do that to him. Hell, he's come all the way from San Francisco to San Coronado." Mac glanced at his watch. "He's supposed to be here by now."

"He's a little late. He's from Ireland. Maybe he's not used to driving on the right side of the road."

"We'd be on the wrong side according to him," Mac said, pausing to turn to her.

The front doorbell rang and he stared into Emma's eyes. "You answer it."

"All right," she said.

Ian Stephens had contacted Mac just thirty-six hours after Emma had posted an open address to the site. Twelve hours later, he was on a plane from Shannon Airport in western Ireland to San Francisco. It hadn't given Mac much of a chance to prepare for the changes that were about to come. Ian had promised him news about his family, about his mother, who was indeed a Quinn, and his older brother.

Emma came back into the room, holding a huge floral arrangement. "It wasn't him," she said.

"More flowers?"

Emma shrugged. "Librarian appreciation week," she said. "The board members must be especially grateful this year."

Mac frowned. "What? Why aren't they sending them to the library?"

She glanced away. "Oh, some of them have. I suppose they just want me to enjoy a couple of bouquets at home, too."

The doorbell rang again and Emma set the arrangement down on the dining room table. "I'll get it."

"If it's more flowers, leave them outside," Mac said. "It's beginning to smell like a funeral parlor in here."

But as he listened to her open the front door, Mac realized that it was Ian Stephens who had arrived. He heard Emma introduce herself and invite him inside. Mac wiped his palms on the front of his shirt. Why was he so nervous?

Stephens entered the room and as soon as he saw Mac, he held out his hand. "Mr. MacKenzie. It's such a pleasure to meet you. I bring greetings from my employer, Miss Aileen Quinn, and from the entire Quinn clan."

Mac nodded and shook the man's hand firmly. He was tall and slender, wearing a finely tailored suit. The kind of guy who probably had never gotten his hands dirty changing a carburetor or rebuilding a fuel pump. "Hi," Mac murmured.

"Would you like to sit in here?" Emma asked.

"Actually, it might be better if we sit at a table," Ian said.

"Why don't we use the one in the dining room?" Emma suggested. "Follow me."

She cleared off a few of the flower arrangements from the table. "I'll just get something for us to drink. I hope lemonade is all right."

"I'd rather have a whiskey," Mac said. "Just bring the bottle."

"Whiskey would be fine for me, too," Ian added.

Emma disappeared into the kitchen as Ian took a place across from Mac. "I know you're probably a bit apprehensive about all this, but let me just assure you that we have been searching for you since the moment we learned of your existence."

Emma returned with the whiskey and two tumblers filled with ice. She set one in front of each of them and added a good measure of whiskey. "Is there anything else I can get you?"

"Sit," Mac said.

"Is it all right if I stay?" Emma asked Ian.

"That's entirely up to Mr. MacKenzie," Ian said.

Mac held out his hand and she laced her fingers into his and sat in the chair beside him. Mac took a deep breath. "I guess we can begin."

Ian reached into his briefcase and pulled out a rolled paper. He removed the rubber band and spread the paper out in front of Mac. "Let's begin with a simple family tree and go from there. At the top, we find Aileen and her four brothers. You're descended from Lochlan Quinn. He's your grandfather. That makes Aileen your great-aunt. Lochlan married Frannie O'Toole and they had one daughter, Mary Therese Quinn. Your mother." He held out a photo and Mac took it from his fingers.

"My mother? This is her? Born in 1955?"

"Yes," Ian said.

"This doesn't look anything like my mother."

"The woman you remember as your mother wasn't your birth mother," Ian explained. "You were given up for adoption right after you were born. Mary Quinn Cassidy already had a young son, and her husband had recently deserted her. Her employer made arrangements for you to be adopted by an older couple, a judge and his wife, and in turn, she'd be allowed to keep her job as a housekeeper."

"He forced her," Mac said.

"Yes. But at least she knew where you were, for the first two years of your life, anyway. She always intended to tell you as soon as you were old enough to understand. But the judge got himself into trouble a few years later, and to avoid going to jail, he and his wife decided to run. They were killed in a car accident near Las Vegas when you were three. You were the only survivor."

"So who were the people that I remember as my parents?" Mac asked.

"We believe they were your foster parents," Ian said. "You were placed with them soon after the accident, but then all three of you disappeared a few months later. Our records show that their names were Fred and Deirdre Reynolds, but we're not sure that's a valid name."

"They were grifters," Mac said. "They probably took me because they needed another body to add to their crime family. They tried to train me to help them cheat people."

"I'm sure we'd be able to track them down if we worked at it."

"I don't ever want to see them again," Mac said. "What was my real name?"

"Judge Cooper and his wife named you Spencer. Mary didn't have the chance to name you, but said that if she had, she would have called you Lukas. That's what she told her older son, Devin, before we knew who or where you were."

"Devin? He would be my brother?"

"Yes," Ian said.

"Where do they live?"

"Mary and Devin live in a small town in North Carolina called Winchester. They're both very anxious to meet you."

Emma gave his hand a squeeze and Mac reached for the glass of whiskey and took a long swallow. "And you're sure I'm your guy?"

"Quite sure," Ian said. "The DNA proves it. Of course we'll double check, but I have every confidence that you will be declared a direct descendant of Lochlan Quinn. As such, you will be entitled to claim part of the large inheritance that Aileen is distributing among her new family members."

"Why would she give me money?" Mac asked. "She doesn't know me."

"I'm authorized to give you half of the money as soon as a follow-up DNA test is confirmed. We can take care of that tomorrow. We have a lab in San Francisco."

Ian pulled a familiar test kit from his briefcase and handed it to Mac. After rubbing the swab on the inside of his cheek, Mac handed the swab and the tube back to Ian.

"Aileen will give you the other half of the inheritance when you visit her."

"I don't have the money for a plane—"

"Oh, no worries," Ian said. "Aileen pays all expenses since the visit is at her request. For you and a guest."

"It'll just be him," Emma said.

"Just me," Mac said.

"Do you have any questions?" Ian asked.

Mac shook his head. "It's all a little hard to digest."

"I understand. Most of the descendants that I deal with are only just learning about the inheritance. You also have to cope with discovering a family you never knew you had." Ian withdrew an envelope from his briefcase. "Your mother and brother sent along some photos for you. They would like to contact you, if that's all right."

"I want to visit them," Mac said. "As soon as possible."

"They'll be thrilled to hear that." Ian stood. "I'm staying at the motel in town for the night and will head back to San Francisco in the morning to confirm the DNA with the lab. Once that's done, I'll issue a check for you and we can proceed."

"I have a birth certificate now," Mac said. "I can get a passport."

"Yes. Your mother sent us a copy of your birth certificate when we started our search for you. It's in the envelope. And I'd suggest that you get a passport quickly. Aileen is very excited about meeting you."

Ian held out his hand and Mac shook it. "I can't tell you how happy we are that we've found you. I hope you feel the same."

"I do," Mac said. "Thank you."

Mac stood at the table and watched the Englishman walk out of the house. Then he closed his eyes and sat back down on the dining room chair. He rubbed his face with his hands.

"I barely remember anything he said," Mac murmured. "I felt like I was inside a bubble."

"I took notes," Emma said, standing beside him.

Mac wrapped his arms around her waist and pressed his cheek to her belly. "Thank you for staying with me."

Emma ran her fingers through his hair and hugged him. "I'm glad I was here."

"I have a birth certificate," he said.

"Do you want to look at it?"

Mac picked up the envelope and withdrew the contents. The birth certificate was on top. "'Baby Boy Cassidy,'" he read. He leaned back and closed his eyes. "You think my name really was going to be Lukas?"

"If it wasn't, then your mother was just trying to make you feel better. And that's a good thing. It means she cares about your feelings."

"Yeah," Mac said. "You're right."

"Why don't you grab that whiskey and let's sit out on the porch and watch the sunset."

"Why don't you grab that whiskey and take me to bed," Mac suggested. "I don't want to think about this right now. I need some serious distraction."

Emma smiled and grabbed the bottle of whiskey. “Is that what I am?” she asked, strolling toward the bedroom. “A distraction?”

“Sweetheart, you are the most distracting distraction I’ve ever known.”

When she reached the bed, Mac came up behind her, smoothing his hands over her hips and her belly, the warmth of her body seeping through the fabric of her skirt and blouse. She arched against him, her soft backside pressed into his lap.

It never took him more than a moment with her to become aroused. This moment was no different. Desperate to feel more, he reached down and unfastened his jeans, freeing the erection that was now at its peak.

Emma reached back and wrapped her fingers around him, beginning a gentle stroke that would lead him to his release. Mac loved the way she touched him, without any hesitation or embarrassment. For her, sex was only what the two of them had experienced together, and she’d learned to be as bold and demanding as he was.

His hands dropped lower as he began to move against her, the fabric of her skirt providing a tantalizing friction. Slowly, he drew her skirt up, exposing her bare legs and the scrap of satin that she was wearing beneath.

She was already aroused, her body grinding against his, looking for more pressure to satisfy her. Mac pulled aside her panties and gently massaged the damp spot between her legs.

Emma moaned as he entered her, leaning back until he was buried to the hilt. He held her waist, keeping her still for a moment while a wave of desire washed over him. Mac drew a ragged breath and focused on the spot where they were joined, on the exquisite sensations that raced through his body when she shifted against him.

He gently positioned her until he could move freely. Slowly, he began to stroke, withdrawing almost completely before plunging inside her. He lost himself in the pleasure her body provided.

This was what he'd always craved, but had never experienced before Emma. Making love to her was about more than just pleasure and release. It was a way to communicate, to strip bare all his fears and vulnerabilities and show Emma who he really was.

And he was a man who needed her love and affection, a man who dreamed of one day offering her the stars and the moon, a man who couldn't imagine a future without her in it.

Another wave of pleasure washed over him and Mac knew that he was close. Emma fell forward onto the edge of the bed and he followed, never breaking their intimate connection.

Tearing aside the fabric of her skirt, he reached around her and found the spot between her legs that sparked her release. His fingers slipped between the damp folds and he gently rubbed, creating a friction that caused her to cry out.

Together, they moved toward the edge, each heartbeat bringing them closer, making the climb exquisite torture. And when he felt her body shudder, Mac let go, falling along with her into a riot of spasms that seemed endless and exhausting.

After the last of their pleasure had passed, Emma pushed up on her elbows and glanced around. "We didn't even bother to get undressed."

"I know. It was kind of sexy," Mac said.

She flopped back down on the bed. "The things you do to me," she murmured. "You've turned me into a very naughty girl."

Mac leaned forward and pressed his lips to the curve of her neck. "You're *my* naughty girl," he whispered. "And that's all that matters."

THE RAIN DRUMMED on the roof of Emma's bungalow, a distant rumble of thunder shaking the old glass in the windows. Emma snuggled into Mac's warm, naked body, inhaling the scent of his skin.

She wanted to commit every detail of him to memory. He'd be gone soon, and all she'd have left were faint images in her head.

"Are you smelling me?" he asked.

Emma giggled. "I didn't realize you were awake."

"I haven't fallen asleep," he said.

Pushing up on her elbow, Emma gazed down into his red-rimmed eyes. "Are you all right?"

"Not so much," Mac said. "I've spent my entire life pushing the past away, convincing myself that it didn't matter. It was easier that way, and I thought it was a pretty healthy choice considering everything I'd been through. But I never reckoned that my past would catch up with me."

"What do you want to do?" Emma asked.

"I want to run away," he said. "Get in my plane and fly as far away from the Quinns as possible. Yesterday,

I even looked at charts for the Pacific. Though whether the Beaver could make it all the way to Hawaii on one tank of fuel is highly doubtful. So, if I want to run, I have to stick to the continental US. But hey, I'll have a passport in a few weeks and a half million to buy a plane ticket to anywhere."

"You don't have to do anything you don't want to do," Emma said.

He sighed. "No, Em, I can't keep avoiding it. I'm a grown man. I have a mother who wants to meet me. And a brother. Do you know how many times I wished for a brother when I was a kid? It's time for me to do the hard work, and I can't be a coward about it. And you're the one who made me face it. Thank you."

Emma leaned forward and brushed a kiss across his lips. It was difficult to absorb the fact that she'd had a direct hand in making him leave. But he'd never be able to have future with her until he faced his past. And she'd never be able to believe in that future until she lived for herself.

"Did you figure out how long it would take to fly the Beaver to Winchester, North Carolina?"

He nodded. "J.J. and I mapped it out."

"Sounds like you have a plan," Emma said. "When are you going to leave?"

"Not for a few days. I have to fly over to Lodi to check out an investment opportunity."

"Spending your money already?" she asked.

"It's actually something I've been thinking about for a while," he said. "An old buddy of mine has a produce farm. He grows organic heirloom vegetables and herbs for the markets in San Francisco. He's looking for a partner."

"You'd settle down?"

"Maybe," Mac said. "If I had a good reason."

A long silence hung between them and Emma wondered what he wanted her to say. Was she supposed to be the reason? Was he trying to tell her that he wanted a future with her? But she couldn't be the reason he changed his life, any more than he could be the reason she'd changed hers.

"It sounds like an interesting opportunity," she said. "I'm going to get us coffee. Do you want toast?"

"I would love toast," he said. "And eggs, too. Or pancakes? Maybe French toast." He swung his legs off the edge of the bed. "I'll make it. You go back to sleep for a bit."

"I'll make it worth your while," she said.

"Oh, now that sounds intriguing," he said. "What time to you have to be at work?"

Emma's breath caught in her throat. She wasn't sure how long she could keep the news of her resignation from Mac. From what she could tell, the board members had decided to keep it confidential, hoping they'd be able to convince her to come back before their part in the mess was exposed.

"I took the day off," she said. "I figured you might need me after your visit with Ian Stephens."

"I need you all the time," he said as he pulled on his jeans.

Emma watched him walk out of the room. "The master of the double entendre," she murmured to herself. "Now what was that supposed to mean? That you want to have sex with me all the time? Or that you actually need me? Because I can't read your mind."

Emma flopped back on the bed and covered her eyes with her arm. There were so many things left unsaid between them, and yet Emma still held her tongue. There were moments when telling him she loved him seemed like the simplest thing in the world. And then, she'd second-guess herself and hold back.

She was in love—crazy, stupid, undeniable love. She wanted to believe that he felt the same and read everything he said and did through the filter of her love-shaded glasses. So the reason he was considering investing in the farm was because he wanted to settle down and make a life for the two of them.

But then she'd examine his choice all over again and find a different meaning. He might have no intention of settling down and working on an organic farm. By investment he might mean just money and nothing else.

Mac was making plans, but Emma wasn't far behind on her own plans. Now that she'd quit as the town librarian, she had the chance to revisit her dreams. There were so many places she'd wanted to explore around the world. She couldn't possibly commit to someone until she'd had her chance for a bit of an adventure.

Thunder rumbled again, now a bit closer. She curled up beneath the blankets, pulling them up to her nose. But as she relaxed in the warmth leftover from his body, Emma heard Mac's footsteps in the hallway. She peeked out from the edge of the quilt to see him standing in the bedroom doorway, a flower arrangement in his arms and a shoebox in the other.

"I found this sitting on the porch," he said. "More flowers courtesy of Librarian Appreciation Week?"

"Must be," she said. "What's in the box?"

"Homemade cinnamon rolls. They're still warm."

"Oh, bring them here," she said, sitting up in bed and patting the mattress beside here. "If I'm right, these are from Madge Belton. She wins lots of awards at the county fair for her cinnamon rolls."

Mac sat down beside Emma and handed her the box. "In fact, they are from Madge. So are the flowers. She left a little note on the top of the box. Do you want to hear what it says?"

Emma sucked in a sharp breath. "No, you don't have to read it."

He grabbed it from his pocket and slowly unfolded it. Emma wanted to snatch it out of his hand, but she checked her impulses.

"'To Emma. Have a happy Librarian Appreciation Day.'"

"Librarian Appreciation Week," Emma corrected.

"Ah, you're right."

"That's not what it says," she admitted.

"No. What it does say is 'On behalf of the ladies of the Library Board, please accept our heartfelt apologies. We sincerely hope that you will retract your resignation. San Coronado needs you, Emma!'" He held out the note. "Look at that. She put an exclamation point at the end. That must mean that she's really serious." Mac pushed off the bed. "Are you going to tell me what's going on?"

Emma reached for a cinnamon bun and he pulled

the box away. She arched her brow and sent him a warning glare.

"Don't look at me like that," he said.

"Give me the box," she demanded.

"Give me an explanation," he countered.

Emma rolled her eyes. This wasn't going to go well. But revealing his part in it would only make him angrier. "I decided that it was time for me to step down. I've learned something from you about living in the present. I want to get out and see a little bit of the world." She paused. "It's a good thing."

"But I don't understand why the board is trying to apologize to you. What did they do to make you resign?"

"We just had a minor argument over policy. And I realized that I didn't want to deal with petty problems for the rest of my life. I wanted to *live* my life."

"What policy?"

"It doesn't make a difference," Emma explained. "Now give me one of those rolls. I'm starving and you're just being cruel."

Reluctantly he handed her the box. "I'm going to go get some coffee. I put a pot on."

"Bring some butter, too," Emma said. Once again, she waited for Mac to leave the room, then relaxed against the headboard. She hoped Mac had believed her. The last thing he needed right now was to take the blame for her quitting her job.

Emma could rest her decision at his feet, but not in a negative way. He was just the spark that had lit the fire. She'd kept her real feelings so deeply hidden over the years that even she didn't know they were there.

Mac had opened her mind and her heart to all the possibilities that her life might offer. But he wasn't the only one who'd tried to teach her that lesson. Emma's mother, Elaine Bryant, had begged her to leave San Coronado and find a more exciting life. But Emma had stubbornly refused. How could she leave her mother when she was dying? But now she owed it to her mother to finally take that advice and run with it.

Mac returned with a tray, balancing the coffee, two plates and the butter dish. He set the tray down on the bed, then handed her a mug. "Thank you," she murmured.

"No problem," he replied.

An uneasy silence descended around them.

"I know you think I resigned because of you," she said. "That maybe now I'll want to come with you when you leave."

He watched her over the rim of the mug, then slowly lowered it. "Do you?"

Emma shook her head. "You need to figure out the rest of your life on your own. And so do I. That doesn't mean that I'm not grateful for what you've done for me. You opened my eyes to so many things. You rescued me from a life that I thought I wanted, but was really very far from what I truly want."

"What are you going to do?"

"I'm planning a trip to Paris," Emma said. "Trisha has a nice long Christmas break and we've always talked about traveling together."

"I've never been to Paris," he said.

"I've been paging through travel books for years

and years. Now I'm finally going to see some of the things listed inside."

She picked a cinnamon roll out of the box and took a big bite of it. "I will miss this, though."

"Homemade cinnamon rolls?"

Emma shook her head. "No. Rainy mornings in bed with you."

"We'd better make it a good one, then," he said.

And, as always, Mac was true to his word.

9

"WHAT ARE YOUR plans now that you're filthy rich?" J.J. asked.

Mac removed the engine cowl from the Beaver and set it on the hangar floor. "A million dollars doesn't go that far these days. If it were just me, I could live on it for the rest of my life."

"But it's not just you?"

Mac shrugged. "Might not be."

"So you and Emma are doing all right?"

"I'm not sure. We really don't talk about the future—ever. I'm not sure if we're avoiding the subject or neither of us has anything significant to say."

"But you do," J.J. said.

"Let's just say I have a vague idea of what a future might be like with Emma. It's just a feeling I get when I'm with her. I know it would be good, I'm just not sure how it would work. And now that Emma quit her job at the library, she—"

"That was a bad deal," J.J. muttered, shaking his head. "Now that folks are finding out the truth, let me tell you, they're pretty damn angry. And I 'spose you can't be too happy to get pulled into it." J.J. cursed softly. "Silly old biddies. They should mind their own business."

"What are they saying?" Mac asked, keeping his tone casual.

"Way I heard it they ganged up on Emma in a private board meeting and warned her that her behavior was unsuitable for the town librarian and that she had to stop seeing you. They called you a drifter."

"Yeah," he murmured. "What did she say?"

"She told them to stuff it," J.J. said. "She quit on the spot. That says a lot about how she feels about you. She wouldn't have given up her job if she wasn't really angry over the way they were talking about you."

Mac leaned against the plane. Emma had left a few key details out of the story she'd given him. Why would she neglect telling him the truth? Would she ever regret what she'd done?

"Is anyone here hungry?"

J.J. grinned as he recognized Emma's voice calling through the hangar. She found them a few moments later, a picnic basket hung over her arm. "Hi, guys," she said.

"Emma," J.J. replied. "Heard your big news. Guess you have time to make picnic lunches now."

"I do," she said, setting the basket down and opening the top. She held out a sandwich, wrapped in waxed paper, to J.J. along with a small container of pasta salad. "I have brownies for dessert," she added.

"I'm just going to go eat this in the office," he said. "I don't wanna be a third wheel."

Emma withdrew another sandwich and held it out to Mac. He took it from her outstretched hand and then sat down beside her. "Thanks," he said.

"No problem." She glanced around. "What are you working on?"

"I'm just giving the plane a good check," he said. "I'm leaving for Winchester at dawn tomorrow to meet my mother and brother."

Emma blinked in surprise. "Tomorrow? That's so soon. Why didn't you tell me?"

He chuckled softly. "We don't tell each other everything, do we? We both have our own secrets."

A frown wrinkled her brow. "What do you mean? I'm honest with you."

"Are you? Because I just found out what really happened at that meeting with the library board. J.J. gave me the whole story. Why didn't you?"

"It wasn't a big deal. Your name came up."

"You failed to mention that. So, tell them you'll take your job back. They obviously realize they made a mistake. Your house is filled with flowers and cinnamon buns."

"I'm not going back," she said.

"But they were right, Emma. I'm not good for you. I am a drifter. And you deserve someone better."

"Stop it!" she said. "I'm not going to listen to you if you talk like that."

"That doesn't mean it isn't true."

"Do you want the truth? All right, here's some truth. I did quit because of you. But not for the reasons they were using. I quit because you showed me I needed to change my life. Not because it was unseemly to be sleeping with you when we weren't married. Do you really think I'm going to listen to those old busybodies? Besides, they wanted me to marry Charlie Clemmons, and we all know what a disaster that would have been." She took a bite of her sandwich. "Satisfied?"

Mac wasn't sure. Her explanation made perfect sense. And yet he still wasn't convinced he was getting the whole truth. Or maybe he was just determined to pick a fight with her, no matter what the cause.

He wanted to shake her up, to get something from her besides blind passivity. What did she want? Was she truly so coldhearted that she wanted nothing beyond what she'd originally requested—no-strings sex? Or was she just trying to protect herself from being abandoned by a guy that everyone called a drifter?

He certainly knew how that worked. Mac had spent a lifetime running away. As long as he could control his exit, then he could never be left behind. And once he was gone, it was so easy to stay away, to keep his heart safe.

"I've always lived my life to please someone else," Emma said softly. "I took the job at the library because it was convenient and I could stay close to my mother when she was ill. I should have left town after she died, but everyone tried so hard to convince me to stay. I couldn't say no."

Damn, he wanted more from her, too. Just like the folks in town. He wanted to tell her that he was falling in love with her and he wanted her to ask him to stay. He wanted to forget everything in their pasts that made it difficult to put those words together. But still, the fears ran deep.

Could he be the kind of man she needed, wanted? He may have a million dollars, but he'd never put down roots. How long would it be before he was itching to move along again? Somehow, Mac suspected that simply loving her would not be enough.

"When I was little, I used to love the Madeline books," she said. "Did you ever read those books?"

He shook his head. "I was more of a Dr. Seuss kid. At one time, I could recite almost all the books from memory. It made it easy when we were between library cards."

"Madeline is a little girl who lives in Paris and goes to a boarding school and she has all these wonderful adventures. My mother loved her, too, and we used to talk about going to Paris together and seeing the place where Madeline lived. It was a wonderful fantasy." He saw tears begin to build in her eyes, and Emma took a quick drink of her soda.

"Are you all right?"

She waved her hand in front of her eyes. "I always get emotional when I talk about my mom." Emma drew a deep breath. "So, when she was dying, I read her the Madeline books and we talked about our dream of going to Paris together. And she made me promise that I'd go—without her. And I promised."

Mac reached out and pulled her into his arms, giving her a hug.

"We really don't have to fight like this," Emma said. "We can just say goodbye and be done with it."

He glanced down at her and took in her watery eyes. "I don't want to fight," he said.

"We can just accept this for what it was. A sweet

but short romantic affair. It doesn't have to turn into love or marriage. It can be a moment in time, just as we agreed in the beginning."

She smiled at him and he saw the truth in her words. She didn't want more from him. Emma had made a plan for her future and it didn't include him. And he was happy for her. She deserved excitement and adventure. There would be another man who would catch her eye and capture her heart. But he wasn't the one.

"So Paris," he said.

"Paris," she replied, her smile widening. "Trisha and I are leaving right after Christmas. The holidays are usually a hard few weeks for me. But this year is going to be different because I have plans!"

"Are you going to sell your house?"

Emma shook her head. "It's paid for, and I need somewhere to keep my stuff. It's home. What about you? Where is home going to be for you?"

"I guess, technically, it would be Winchester, North Carolina. I now have an official hometown."

"You need to get a passport," she said.

"That's on my list, too," he said.

"Who knows, maybe we'll run into each other out there in the big wide world."

"I sure hope so," Mac said.

They finished up their picnic lunch and Emma started packing it up to leave. Mac realized this would be the last time he saw her. After all they'd been through, what they had would end here, in the hangar, just a few feet from where it began.

Mac wrapped his arms around her. "Have a great trip to Paris," he said. "Send me a postcard."

"I will," Emma promised. "And if you ever come back this way again, call me. I'll make you dinner."

Mac watched her walk away, then moved to the overhead door of the hangar and tracked her car until it was out of sight.

"Did she leave already?" J.J. asked, stepping up to his side.

"Yeah, she had to go."

"I thought she had brownies."

Mac turned and pointed to the remains of his lunch. "She left them for you."

J.J. crossed his arms over his chest. "I didn't think you'd let her go."

"I've got a lot to figure out in my own life, J.J. Now is not the best time to invite another person along for the ride."

"Even if you love her?"

"Especially if I love her," Mac said.

EMMA CLIMBED THE front steps of the library, smiling to herself as she reached the entrance. She hadn't been inside since the day she quit, but now, necessity had called. There was one person she had to see.

As she strolled through the lobby, she waved at two of her former employees, now hard at work behind the circulation desk, helping the after-school crowd with their selections.

Lily Harper was sitting in her usual place, books spread out over the large library table. A young girl sat across from her, her nose buried in a Nancy Drew mystery.

"Hello, Lily," Emma said, sitting down next to her.

"Miss Bryant. Hi." Emma saw a real smile break through the girl's normally solemn expression. "Where have you been? They told me you quit."

"I did."

"Didn't you like your job?" Lily asked.

"I loved my job. But I realized it was time I chased some of my dreams. And I couldn't do both."

"You're going to chase your dreams?"

Emma nodded. "I'm taking a trip to Paris," she said. "I'm leaving right after Christmas."

"Where Madeline lives," Lily said.

"Yes, that's right."

"I've read all the Madeline books," Lily said.

"Me, too," the other girl added.

"This is Daisy Lopez," Lily said. "She's my friend from school. She likes the library, too."

"Daisy and Lily? Oh, you two were meant to be best friends, weren't you?"

Both girls nodded, grinning at each other. "We are friends," Daisy said. "Lily told me about Nancy Drew." The other girl pushed back from the table. "I just finished this one. Now I have to go get the next book."

"The Mystery at Lilac Inn," Lily said.

Daisy skipped off into the children's section and Emma turned back to Lily. "I heard that you're going through with the adoption."

Lily nodded. "Denise arranged for me to visit my mother. She's in prison and she's not going to get out for a long time. But she said that she wanted me to have a good life, to be safe, so that she wouldn't have to worry about me. We write to each other and I send her things. And it's all right with Dave and Denise. We talk about it a lot."

"Have you been using your library card?" Emma asked.

Lily giggled. "Yeah. I had an overdue book yesterday. I owed a nickel but they said I didn't have to pay."

"Good," Emma said. "If I were still running the place, I'd let you go, too."

"Are you ever going to come back?"

"I'm not sure. Maybe. But for now, I'm going to have some adventures. And I'll send you some postcards."

"That'd be cool," Lily said. "And thanks. For helping me. I was really sad when I came here and now I like it. I'm going to have a mom and a dad. And maybe a little sister."

"A sister?"

"Yeah. We have another foster child and she might get adopted, too. Her name is Renee."

"You'll make a wonderful big sister." Emma leaned in and gave Lily a hug. "You study hard and I'll see you when I get back."

"Sure," Lily said. "We can have lunch."

A month ago, Lily had been just another patron, a sad and lonely girl who sat alone in the library. But Emma had tried to find answers for her, and when she did, a whole new world had opened up for the girl.

Emma had done that for Mac, too. She'd helped him discover the kind and sweet and loving man he truly was. She'd helped him find his mother and brother and a whole family of Quinns just waiting for him to join them.

She felt like a mother bird, shoving her chicks out

of the nest for the first time and encouraging them to fly away on their own adventures.

Emma turned, walked out into the November afternoon and drew a deep breath of the cool air. She glanced at her watch, then hurried to her car.

The travel agency was only a few blocks away and when she pulled up to the curb, she noticed Trisha's car was already parked out front. They had an appointment to go over the arrangements for their Paris trip.

Emma hurried inside and found Trisha and Frannie Hillberger sitting at a desk, Frannie's attention fixed on the computer screen in front of her. "There's a nonstop flight on Air France that leaves at two in the afternoon on the twenty-sixth."

"Sure," Emma said. "That sounds good."

"Nonstops are always better," Trisha said. "Fewer ups and downs."

"How long is the flight?" Emma asked.

"Just under eleven hours," Frannie said. "There's an Air Lingus flight that stops in Dublin, but if you're already in Dublin it isn't that much farther to Paris."

"I've always wanted to see Ireland," Emma said.

"Your friend, Luke MacKenzie, was in this morning. He exchanged a voucher for a ticket to Ireland."

"He's still around?" Emma said. "I—I thought he'd left town."

Frannie shrugged. "He's coming back to pick up his ticket tomorrow, so I guess he is still around. Do you have any preference for seat assignment?"

"Away from crying babies," Trisha said. "And chatty children?"

"I'm afraid I can't control that. Unless you want to book in first class."

"How much is that?" Emma asked.

"Almost triple the price," Frannie said.

"I can't afford first class," Trisha said.

"But I can. This is my first trip and I intend to make it memorable. When I think back on this, I want to have wonderful memories. Trisha, I'll pay for the upgrade. I've been saving money for years and now I'm going to start spending it."

"Em, I can't accept—"

"Of course you can." She turned to Frannie. "Now, what else?"

"I have some hotels for you to look at. I think you'll be really happy with this one—Hotel Fleurie. It's small and intimate, but quite luxurious. It offers separate rooms, as you requested, and it's reasonably priced for central Paris. It's located on the Left Bank in the sixth arrondissement. Saint-Germain-des-Prés."

"Did you hear that, Emma? The sixth arrondissement! I have no idea what that means, but we're going to Paris! We're going to Paris!" Trisha threw her arms around Emma's neck and hugged her. "We're going to have so much fun."

Emma looked at the photos on Frannie's screen, then nodded. "I like it. Trish, what about you?"

"We could sleep in a Dumpster and I'd be happy. It's Paris!"

"Book it," Emma said.

"Airport transportation. Though it's a bit more expensive than a cab, I'd recommend a private car and driver. It will be prepaid, so you won't have to worry about changing money until you get settled in your hotel."

"That sounds perfect," Emma said.

"Perfect," Trisha agreed.

"Is that all?" Emma asked.

Frannie nodded. "For now. I'll make these arrangements and then you'll need to come back in and pay for everything. At that time I can show you some tour options. There's a nice château tour, as well as vineyard tours and cooking tours. So many things to do."

Emma quickly stood. "Fine. We'll talk about that when we come in next. Thanks, Frannie."

She hurried to the door and Trisha ran after her. When she reached the street, Emma drew a long breath and tried to calm her racing pulse. He was still in town. For the past three days she'd stubbornly put Mac out of her mind, convincing herself that what they'd decided was the best for both of them.

"He's still in town?" Emma said, grabbing on to Trisha when she reached her side.

"I wasn't sure if I should tell you. You were doing so well. I saw J.J. yesterday and he said that Mac had some trouble with the plane and he has to wait for a new part to come in before he can leave. He's been laying low."

"He doesn't want to see me," Emma said.

"You can't be sure of that."

"He hasn't tried to contact me."

"You said your goodbyes. Maybe he didn't want to put either of you through that again."

Emma covered her eyes and groaned. Three days. She'd been imagining him in North Carolina getting to know his family. She'd even searched for the street view of his mother's house so that she could have the right picture in her head.

"Are you mad that I didn't say something to you?" Trisha asked.

"Of course not. If you had, these last three days would have been torture. As it is, I just have a day until he finally leaves."

"Why don't you just tell him how you feel?" Trisha asked. "Put it out there. See what he says. You don't have anything to lose."

"But he does," Emma said. "He's got so much going on right now, so many things he needs to do. The guy just found out he has a family and a million dollars. I'm not sure he'd even know how he truly felt."

"You're making excuses for him?" Trisha asked.

"No. I'm trying to empathize with all that he's going through. And look at me. I could use a little perspective, too. He's the first guy I've ever slept with. My own feelings might be a bit clouded. We both need a little space."

"You could tell him you'll meet him on top of the Empire State Building on Valentine's Day."

"That was taken from *An Affair to Remember*. Cary Grant and Deborah Kerr."

"Remade by Warren Beatty and Annette Bening," Trisha said.

"I used to watch those movies and imagine that if I could just have one romance in my life, just a few weeks of perfect bliss, that I'd be satisfied. That I could live the rest of my life happy."

"It doesn't work that way," Trisha said.

"No, it doesn't. Why didn't you tell me that?"

Trisha shrugged. "You had a nice little fantasy going there. I didn't want to spoil it." She grabbed Emma's arm. "Come over to my place for a glass of wine. I ordered some Paris guidebooks from Amazon and they were supposed to come today."

"Perfect, something to distract me," Emma said. "If I say anything about driving out to the airport to see Mac, promise me that you'll tie me up and lock me in your bathroom."

"I promise," Trisha said.

MAC SAT IN the shadows of Emma's porch, the chilly night air seeping through his jacket. It was almost eleven and she'd yet to return home. It wasn't like Emma to stay out late at night. But then, she wasn't working anymore, so there really was no reason to get home early.

He pushed to his feet and began to pace the length of the porch in an attempt to warm up. She'd shown him where she kept the key and, a few weeks ago, he wouldn't have thought twice about letting himself inside and making himself comfortable.

But they'd called an end to their relationship a few days ago and he didn't want to make assumptions. It had been difficult enough to spend his days in San Coronado, knowing she was there, just a phone call or a short drive away. And he'd managed to avoid temptation—until tonight.

The need to see her again was just too much to deny. Mac was aware of all the reasons why it was wrong. They'd said their goodbyes already and he'd accepted that they were both going to walk away without any plans for the future.

But as the days passed and he'd had a chance to think, Mac realized it was going to be impossible to live with the uncertainty of their decision. He needed to know that he'd see her again, that she'd welcome him back into her life once he'd cleaned up the chaos in his past.

Mac understood that he was taking a risk. He had no idea how Emma felt about him and that had been his fault.

Throughout their short but very intense relationship, Mac had been careful not to allow himself to express his feelings for her. He'd tried to remember that the relationship was about sex and nothing more. And when his affection for Emma had grown, he'd ignored it, certain that he'd be able to push it aside once they parted ways.

He hadn't expected to fall in love with her. And there was no doubt that he loved her. He had plenty of experience brushing aside casual affection. But in the past few days he'd come to learn that love was an entirely different matter. It was a constant craving that consumed his mind and his heart, his entire body. He couldn't fight it. He didn't want to. It felt far too good.

Just then, her car pulled up in front of the house.

"What are you doing here?" she asked as came to stand beside him.

"I needed to see you just once more. There are some things that I wanted to say to you."

"Mac, I'm not sure—"

He pressed his finger to her lips. "Just let me explain. I've been thinking about this for the last forty-eight hours and I have it all laid out in my head. So, if I can just say it, without interruption, maybe I'll be able to get it right."

Emma held out her hand. "It's chilly out here. How long have you been waiting?"

"About an hour. I assumed you'd be home."

"I was over at Trisha's. I heard you were still in town and I was fighting my own temptations."

Emma drew him into the house. Silently, she helped him out of his jacket then walked with him to her bedroom.

Mac wasn't sure that he was ready to strip off all his clothes and make love to her. It was already almost impossible to imagine leaving. How could he walk away after spending the night, naked in her arms?

To his surprise, though, she stopped after tugging off his shoes. Emma kicked off her own shoes and then crawled beneath the covers on the bed. She held them up in a wordless invitation to join her.

Mac lay down beside her, both of them still completely clothed. It was an odd thing, but it felt right. They were as close as they could be without being naked. They were still vulnerable, intimate, but there was no undercurrent of sexual need. It was the perfect place for the two of them.

"When do you leave?" she asked.

"Tomorrow morning. I had some mechanical problems with the plane, but J.J. and I got them fixed."

"I'm glad. I'd hate to think that there's something wrong with the plane."

"Stuff happens," he said. "A couple weeks ago I had hydraulic problems and had to land in a farm field."

"You didn't mention that," she said.

"It was just a little glitch. I fixed the problem myself and got back in the air after an hour on the ground. I know what I'm doing up there, Em. It's here with you that I feel like an idiot."

She reached out and pressed her palm to his cheek. "You're not an idiot."

"Yes, I am. There are so many things I have to say to you, and I can't seem to figure out how to put them into words."

"We have all night," she said.

He closed his eyes and pulled her closer, pressing a kiss to her forehead. "I never dreamed I'd meet someone who I'd want to spend a lifetime with. I didn't believe in love or commitment. I ran in the other direction when anyone got too close."

"You had a rotten childhood," Emma said.

"I never wanted to blame my childhood," Mac said. "I was a kid. I'm a man now and I should have control of my life. I assumed I was just like every other guy who didn't want to settle down. And I enjoyed being a single guy. I was free to live my life exactly the way I wanted, without anyone to tell me differently."

"You would not be good marriage material," she said.

"That's what I thought. But then I met you and you messed everything up."

"You messed it all up for me, too," she said.

"Em, I don't want this to be the end. But it can't be the beginning. Not yet. I have a lot of things I need to fix in my life before I can figure out what's going on between you and me."

"I know how you feel," she said.

"Do you?"

"I want to travel, I want to experience more of life than I have over the past ten years. I deserve to have a few adventures."

"If we were both ready, I'd marry you tomorrow. But I wouldn't be the guy you deserve. And you wouldn't be ready, either."

"Maybe we should meet each other a year from now. If we both want to move forward we meet at…"

"The Eiffel Tower?" Mac asked.

Emma shook her head.

"The Golden Gate Bridge?"

"No. My front porch," she said. "When you're ready, you come back here, knock on my front door and see if I let you in."

"A year is a long time," he said. "Six months might be better."

"All right. Six months. How about April Fool's Day?"

"No," he said. "Valentine's Day."

"That's only three months away," she said softly.

"Too soon," he said. "All right. A year."

Emma shook her head. "May seventeenth," she said. "It's my birthday."

"All right," Mac said. He leaned forward and kissed her, his lips soft against hers. "It's a plan. May seventeenth on your front porch."

A flood of relief raced through him. He'd gone from

having nothing to having everything he'd ever needed in the blink of an eye. A chance to make this work.

Mac had no doubt that they'd spend the rest of their lives together...eventually. But Emma deserved an adventure of her own, a chance to be the woman that she wanted to be. Something had always held her back: her appearance when she was young, her mother's illness, her gratitude to a town that had watched over her. He couldn't be the one to stop her this time. She'd spent her whole life pleasing others, and as much as he wanted her around to please him, this was her chance to discover the woman she was meant to be.

Mac knew that if they made a commitment now, she'd want to follow him. His dreams would become her dreams. He wouldn't allow Emma to fall into that trap.

"So, I have just one more question," she said.

"Shoot," he said. "I have all the answers."

"What if you meet another woman?"

"I won't," Mac said.

"What if you do?"

"I won't. I don't want anyone but you."

"All right. What if I meet another man?"

Mac pondered the question for a long moment. He already knew the answer but that didn't make it any easier to say. "If you meet someone who you want to kiss then you should kiss him," Mac said.

"All right. And the same goes for you. No strings. It's not going to do us any good to avoid other people. Otherwise, how will we be sure?"

Mac went from feeling pretty great about their plan to pretty rotten. But it was only fair. They both needed to put this relationship in perspective. Was it love or just a passing infatuation? If he felt an attraction to another woman, then he had his answer.

He sat up and swung his legs over the edge of the bed. "I guess I'll see you on May seventeenth," he murmured.

"You can stay the night," she said.

Mac glanced over his shoulder. "I can't. There's no way I'd be able to keep my hands off you."

"Same here," she said.

"Leaving you is going to be hard enough, Em. I don't want to make it worse."

She got up on her knees and hugged him from behind. "Then go."

He shifted on the bed.

"Don't turn around," she warned him.

"I want to kiss you," he murmured.

"You don't need to kiss me," Emma said. "You remember exactly how it feels. And how I taste. You remember it all. It's imprinted on your brain and on your tongue and on your fingertips. Walk away, Mac."

Drawing a deep breath, he stood. Her arms fell away from him and he immediately felt the loss. Mac took one step toward the door and then another.

When he finally reached the front door, he drew a deep breath, then opened it. Though his rational mind assured him that what he was doing was right for them both, Mac's heart was saying something entirely different.

Six months without Emma would be an eternity. But if it all worked out as he hoped, then they'd have forever. And forever with Emma was all he'd ever need.

10

THE PRISON YARD was dry and dusty, the Nevada sun bleaching the paint on the scarred wooden picnic tables. All around him, female prisoners, dressed in standard-issue jumpsuits, were enjoying their visitors—young children, teenagers, spouses and parents.

He waited at one of the tables, wondering what the next hour might bring. For the past few weeks, Mac had been chasing his past. With the help of a private investigator that Ian Stephens had hired and the advice of his brother, Dev, a local police chief, Mac had finally located his foster mother. She was serving the fourth year in a ten-year sentence for fraud.

Mac watched as a slender woman approached, her sandy blond hair hanging around her face. She stopped at his table. "Who are you?" she asked.

"You don't remember me?" he asked.

She stared at him for a long moment, then smiled. "You're the kid," she said.

"Luke MacKenzie," he said.

"Luke? Are you sure? I thought we called you Sean."

He shook his head. "Nope. Luke."

She sat down across from him, an odd grin curling the corners of her hard mouth. Mac was shocked at how different she looked. He remembered her as sweet and beautiful. Life had not been kind to her.

"I never knew your name," Mac said.

"Lorelei," she said. "Lorelei Nelson. I can't remember what I was calling myself when you were with us." She chuckled. "Gosh, you were a cute kid. Smart, too. And look at how you turned out." She paused. "So, you have money?"

Mac shook his head. "No."

"We tried to teach you some useful skills, but you never really took to it. Some kind of ethical streak. Robby could never figure it out. He finally got fed up and we left you in that motel room. You were useless."

"How did you get me in the first place?" Mac asked.

"We needed a kid for some jobs we had planned. People trust a couple with a kid. We set ourselves up in a house, forged a few documents and became foster parents. As soon as we got you, we took off. Your face was on a milk carton for five years before they finally stopped searching for you."

"So you never really cared about me. You just wanted me to help with the cons you pulled."

"I liked you," she said. "You could have been my own kid. Robby wouldn't let me get pregnant. He said it was too risky. If I had a baby, there would be all kinds of questions."

"Where is Robby?"

She shrugged. "We lost track of each other. I wanted to get you back and he didn't. I returned to the motel the next week, thinking you'd still be there, but the cops had gotten you. I watched your school for a while. I figured I could snatch you and we'd be one happy family again."

"Why didn't you?"

She drew a deep breath and stared at a spot beyond his shoulder. "I saw that you were happy. You had a couple of friends. You were learning to play soccer. I figured you deserved a chance. I couldn't give you that, and Robby never wanted to."

"Do you know how to find Robby?" Mac asked.

"He don't want to see you," Lorelei said.

"Do you know how to find him?" he asked again.

She regarded him shrewdly. "How much is it worth?"

"You want cash? Now?"

"In my account. Talk to the guard when you leave. He'll show you how."

"All right. Fifty dollars."

"A hundred," she said.

"All right."

"Robby VanEss. Robert Scott VanEss. He's got a sister who's doing time in Chowchilla. Penelope Van-Ess. And another sister who lives in Truckee by the name of Angela. I think her last name is Rivera."

"I'll check it out. If the info is good, I'll send the money."

She opened her mouth, then snapped it shut. "I be-lieve you. You got that ethical streak inside you. You wouldn't lie." She pulled a pack of cigarettes from her pocket and offered him one, but Mac shook his head. "Gotta light?"

"Nope."

She tossed the pack on the picnic table. "I gotta give 'em up anyway." Lorelei looked at him. "So how are you doing? You got a wife or a girlfriend?"

"A girlfriend," he said.

"Make sure you treat her right. Robby, he never treated me like a wife. I was a way for him to make more money and that was all. I thought he loved me, but I was wrong."

Mac stood and stepped away from the table. "I have to go."

"Yeah. I suppose you won't be coming back, will you?"

Mac shook his head. "No."

"I don't blame you. Sometimes it's just easier to forget the bad parts of your life and move on." She stood and crossed her arms over her chest.

Mac nodded and began to walk away, then remembered one other thing. He turned to face her. "The tin, with the ring and the watch. Do you remember that?"

Lorelei nodded. "Sure. I used to help you hide it."

"Where did it come from? Why did I have it?"

"The social worker told me it was stuff that they got from your parents after the car crash. Their personal stuff. You know, heirlooms."

Mac smiled. He'd carried the tin around all these years only to find out that what it contained had no connection to his birth family at all, just the couple who had taken advantage of a young, desperate woman.

"I'm sorry for what we put you through. I don't expect you to accept my apology," she said. "But I mean it."

"Goodbye, Lorelei. And good luck."

"You, too."

He strode back to the gate, dust kicking up around his shoes and a trickle of sweat running down his temple. Mac wasn't sure what he'd expected from Lorelei, but this wasn't it. The woman he'd once known as his mother was still there behind the hard exterior that life and prison had created. But his memory had held on to all the good things and forgotten the bad. He'd idealized her until she had been like some fairy godmother. In reality, she was a criminal who'd kidnapped a boy at the behest of her abusive spouse.

He walked out the front gate. Devin was waiting for him in Mac's rental car. He opened the door and got inside, the cool interior a relief from the heat outside.

"That was quick," Dev said.

"Yeah. There wasn't much to say." Mac leaned back into the seat. "Thanks for finding her, though. I'm glad I had a chance to talk to her again. I needed to get that straight in my head."

"Did she give you any clues about her husband?"

Mac nodded. "She did. But now I'm not sure I want to see him. I think I'm all right."

Mac had met his brother only a few weeks ago, but they'd already become good friends. He'd spent a week in Winchester, getting to know his mother and brother, as well as Devin's wife, Elodie. They'd done some fishing, played some pool, went flying and ate a lot of barbecue—just the kind of things he'd always imagined doing with a brother.

Dev had been interested in finding the couple who'd kidnapped Mac from the foster system, so he'd gone to work, looking for clues. With what Mac could recall, Dev was able to find the original police report from the abandonment and an old fingerprint report that led him to Lorelei Nelson, an inmate at McClure in Vegas.

"How close are we to San Coronado?" Dev asked as he pulled the car out of the lot.

"Seven or eight hours by car," he said. "A lot less by air."

"It's almost Christmas," Dev said. "Maybe you ought to pay her a visit. Before she heads off to Paris."

There had been a lot of time to talk over ribs and beer, and Dev had been a good listener. They'd argued over Mac and Emma's "plan" that would keep them apart until May—Dev was strongly against it and Mac tried to defend it, though his arguments were getting weaker and weaker.

"I say we spend tonight visiting a few casinos, having a little fun, and then you fly to Cali and I'll head back to North Carolina."

Mac didn't need to think about it for long. He'd put together the pieces of his past. His visit with Lorelei had proved to him that what he'd experienced as a boy was not his fault. At every turn, the adults in his life had made choices that he couldn't change. He hadn't been in control, so like a bottle floating on a vast ocean, he had gone where he was pushed.

But he did have control of his present and his future, and he was determined to make up for the pain of the past. He would live a happy life with the woman he loved. And if they ever had a family, he would fight to the death to protect his own children from the sadness and loss that he'd experienced as a child.

He was finished with the past. There was nothing more to do. He wanted to get on with his future and that future was with Emma.

"THIS IS NICE," Emma said, holding up a men's dress shirt."

"Joey doesn't wear checks," Trisha said.

"I wasn't thinking of it for Joey," Emma said.

"Then who were you thinking of? A certain pilot, perhaps?"

Emma groaned. Trisha knew her far too well. And she'd also been the only person Emma had confided in about Luke MacKenzie.

"Yes, Mac," she said. "This shirt would look fabulous on him. I'm going to buy it for him."

"Didn't you buy him a belt yesterday and a wallet the day before?"

"Yes, but I'm just getting into the Christmas spirit. I don't have anyone but you and Joey to buy for. It would be nice to have a boyfriend around."

"Have you heard from him?"

Emma shook her head. "I'm sure he's with his family for the holidays. It's too soon. He's only been gone six weeks."

"Six weeks is a long time," Trisha said.

"What are you saying?"

"I'm saying it's a long time. Six weeks. Forty-two days. One thousand and eight hours."

"Stop that," Emma said. "You know I think it's creepy when you do that."

"Multiply in my head?"

"No, multiply random stuff until you can't multiply anymore."

"It's a special power," Trisha said. "My students love it. I can recite prime numbers, too."

"Are you going to bother me like this in Paris?"

"Of course not. I'm going to be the perfect traveling companion."

"And you won't bother me if I want to buy something for Mac?"

"No, of course not. I just don't want you to fill your house with stuff like one of those hoarders on television."

"He is going to come back," Emma said.

"Why don't you just admit that you miss him? Why don't you call him and tell him that you love him?"

"He still needs to sort things out. We can't really start a future until he deals with his past."

"Oh, please. He's twenty-seven years old. It's not that hard. Either he loves you or he doesn't. It's a simple question. Do you drink coffee or tea? Do you prefer baths or showers? Do you love Emma Bryant or—or someone else?"

"You're not making me feel better," Emma said.

"Sorry. I'll stop. And I agree that shirt would look great on him, as long as he kept it unbuttoned. Buy it."

Emma took the shirt up to the counter and handed it to the salesgirl. She carefully folded it and put it in a tissue-lined box.

"Would you like a gift receipt?" she asked.

"No."

"Gift wrap?"

"No, just the box is fine."

They walked out to Emma's car and put their purchases in the trunk. She'd already bought a few other things for herself and a few for the absent boyfriend. She liked to imagine that he'd be coming home for Christmas. In her lonely moments she'd almost convinced herself it was true.

San Coronado was decorated for the holidays, with strings of lights and tinsel figurines draped from pole to pole. There was no snow, but a chill in the air added to the ambience.

"Are you sure you don't want to join us for Christmas Eve tonight? My family will be there, and Joey's brothers. It'll be fun."

"I always spend Christmas Eve alone. Just me, a bowl of popcorn and *It's a Wonderful Life*. I wouldn't want to break my tradition. But I will come for dinner tomorrow. I don't have much food in my house. I cleaned out the fridge for our trip."

Emma dropped Trisha off at her apartment, then drove back to her house. As she was pulling the car into the driveway, she noticed someone sitting on her porch. She couldn't see who it was but fervently hoped it wasn't Charlie Clemmons back for one more try.

When she switched off the car, she got out and gathered all her purchases, then walked around to the front of the house. But to her surprise, whoever was sitting on the porch was gone.

"Hello?" Emma called. "Hello?"

"Merry Christmas, Emma."

She spun around to find Mac standing next to her car, his hands braced on his hips, a smile playing on his lips.

"You're here," she cried.

He nodded. "I tried to stay away but I couldn't. And I understand if you still need more time. I'm just going to stand here and look at you for a few more minutes, then I'll be on my way."

"But you just got here," Emma said.

"I don't want to wear out my welcome."

She smiled, shaking her head. "I missed you, too."

"How much?"

"Much more than I ever thought I would. You're constantly on my mind. But May seventeenth isn't that far away, right?"

"It's just so difficult, being without you. Every day, there are a million things I want to tell you, and every night, I wish I was holding you in my arms instead of sleeping alone. And May seventeenth might as well be years away."

"You don't think about the sex?"

"Well, that, too. I'm trying to be romantic here."

Emma giggled. "You're doing a really good job. Keep going."

"That's all I came to say. I suppose if you give me a few more minutes I could come up with some more pretty words, but I got the important stuff out." He shrugged. "Maybe you could say something now."

She'd talked about having adventures, taking risks, but she'd avoided the biggest risk of all—being completely honest with Mac. "I told you from the beginning that this was just about sex. But it wasn't. And it hasn't been for a long time. I fell in love with you and I was too ashamed to admit it to myself. I thought I could make myself immune to your charms, but I couldn't.

So, I'm going to admit my fatal flaw. I'll love you forever, Luke MacKenzie. Or Lukas Cassidy Quinn, or whatever you plan to call yourself. And I will do anything to keep you close to me. You are the life I want."

"Did you say you love me?" Mac asked.

"I did."

"Say it again."

"I love you. I love you, love you, love you."

In a heartbeat, he closed the distance between them and swept her into his embrace, his lips coming down on hers in a deep, demanding kiss. The shopping bags dropped to the ground and Emma wrapped her arms around his neck.

He picked her up off her feet, hugging her so tight she couldn't breathe. Emma laughed, pushing away from him and wriggling back to the ground.

"When do you leave for Paris?"

"We're driving to San Francisco tomorrow night and staying at a hotel. Our flight leaves at noon."

"That gives us less than forty-eight hours."

"For what?"

"Carols, presents, eggnog by the tree and holiday sex. I've never really celebrated Christmas as an adult, but this year I'm going to start."

"I have some presents for you," she said. "I hoped you might come."

"I have just one present for you," he said. Mac pulled her along to the porch and they sat on the wicker chairs, facing each other.

"I've never been a very traditional guy. No one ever taught me how to romance a woman."

"You're doing just fine," Emma said.

"But there is one thing I do know. You don't let the woman you love go off to Paris without telling her exactly how you feel."

"And how do you feel?"

"I love you. And I will love you forever." Mac reached in his jacket pocket and withdrew a ring. "Like I said, I've never been a traditional guy, but these past few weeks, I've discovered that I am. I've discovered exactly who I am and what I want. And I want you to have this right now. You can wear it or you can put it away. It can mean that you want to marry me or it can mean that we'll figure it all out later. This is a token of my deep and undying affection, Emma. Will you accept this ring?"

He opened the box and Emma looked inside. She gasped softly at the cushion cut diamond surrounded by sparkling baguettes.

"If you don't like it, we can take it back and get another."

"It's perfect," she murmured.

He carefully plucked it out of the box and slipped the ring onto her finger. "You're perfect," he replied.

Emma pushed up on her toes and brushed a soft kiss across his lips. "We're perfect together."

He scooped her into his arms and carried her up the front porch steps and into the house. And when they crossed the threshold, Emma felt something deep inside her, something so sure and certain that she could close her eyes and imagine it all happening.

This was her life. Mac was her life. And it was beginning right now.

Epilogue

"MR. STEPHENS, HAVE you been waiting here long?"

Ian stood up as Aileen Quinn entered the room, her ornate wooden cane rapping against the wooden floor. "I've been flipping through your photo album," he said.

Aileen looked over his shoulder and smiled at the photos. "Claire helped with that," she said.

It was a pleasant benefit to have one of her own family, her grandniece, married to her research assistant, Aileen mused. Now, if she could only get the couple to move in with her, her happiness would be complete. Claire had recently given birth to twin girls and they'd become regular visitors at the house—and a welcome respite from the usual tomb-like silence that surrounded her. At eleven months, the twins were both walking and more than a handful.

The older she got, the more Aileen needed the stimulation of the younger generations. Since the various little ones had been coming to visit, she'd forgotten all about her aches and pains. She lived for the chaos they created.

"We could put all of your photos on your tablet and

there would be no need for a photo album," Ian said. "We have over three thousand photos."

"I'm an old-fashioned woman," Aileen said, sitting down in the wing chair next to his. "I prefer a photo album. And I enjoy putting it together with Claire. We choose our favorites and then she prints them off and I paste them in the book. Not everything has to be done by computer."

"And it is a good excuse to see the girls," Ian said with a chuckle. "Oh, I suppose I loathe technology almost as much as you do. There is something wonderful about sitting down with an old-fashioned book and doing research. I find myself in front of my computer for most of the day."

"Oh, I don't loathe technology, Ian. I'm just very suspicious of it. It makes simple human interactions almost obsolete. Like us having tea together. We could text or Skype. You could fax me your report. Or you could come to my home and we could have a lovely cup of tea together. That sounds much more enjoyable to me."

Almost perfectly on cue, tea appeared at the library door. But Aileen was surprised to see Ian's wife, Claire, with the tray instead of her housekeeper, Sally.

"You are here, too? Have you brought Alice and Esme?"

"Not today," Claire said. "They both have colds and I thought it best to quarantine them at home. Marlie agreed to watch them."

"Well, come then. You can sit behind my desk. I'm far too comfortable in this chair to move."

"Sally is going to join us, as well," Claire said. "She's bringing the scones."

A few seconds later, the housekeeper appeared in the doorway with the tea table. She set it between Ian and Aileen, then quickly prepared a plate for Claire and placed it on the desk.

"Why, we have a regular party here," Aileen said. "Certainly we can find something to celebrate."

"Actually, there is something," Ian said. "I guess you could say this is my last official report on our project. We have found the last missing Quinn. The family is now complete." Aileen clapped enthusiastically. "Bravo. Well-done, you. It's been a long road, hasn't it? How long has it been? Three years?"

"Very nearly," Ian said. "In that time, I met my wife, got married and had twin daughters. There were moments when I despaired whether we'd ever be done, Aileen."

"I'm thrilled that you found Lukas. He was a very difficult case, but he'll be coming for his visit soon and then it will be done."

"There's still Lochlan," Ian reminded her.

"I suppose we can't expect to tie up every single loose end." She turned to Claire. "Your grandfather has proved himself a rather tough case, hasn't he. Children on two different continents. Someday, we may learn where he's buried and that will be our epilogue."

Ian handed her a file folder. "I assumed the reason we weren't able to find Lochlan in the US Social Security death index is that he never became a US citizen and therefore was ineligible to collect. But according to Mary, Lochlan's daughter, her father worked at the

Winchester mill. So he must have had work papers, papers that could be traced. So, I hired an expert in immigration affairs and it turns out, there was a long record of Lochlan's work history in the US."

"You found him," Aileen said.

"Better than that," Ian replied. "He's alive and quite well for 105. He lives in a retirement community in San Diego, California."

Aileen stared at Ian, aghast. She'd always hoped that she might find one of her brothers alive. But as the years passed, she'd accepted the fact that the odds were highly against her. And now, after the search for her descendants was over, Ian had found Lochlan—alive!

She didn't know whether to laugh or to cry. "Ian, I—I am afraid—I have no words to express my gratitude. Month after month you've brought me wonderful news, the results of your diligent work. And now this."

"I hope you won't think this too forward, but I've arranged for a private jet. Lochlan doesn't travel, but I was sure that you would, given the circumstances. The trip should be stress-free. Claire and I will accompany you. And Mary, Devin and Lukas will join us for a few days. Are you up to the trip?"

"Oh, yes," Aileen said. "This news has made me feel young again. And if it's the very last thing I do on this earth, I will not regret the decision. Sally, you'll come with us, as well. I'm not sure I can do without you."

"Yes, ma'am."

"We must pack. I suppose for at least a week, perhaps two."

Aileen pressed her hand to her chest and drew a deep breath. "I feel quite rejuvenated. How odd. But you're right. It's a long trip and I must pace myself. I'm not a young woman anymore."

"You must promise me you'll take things slowly," Ian said. "And if at any time you need to rest, you'll speak up."

"I promise," she said.

She'd often wondered how she might react if one of her brothers were found alive. She'd never expected such a riot of emotion. She'd lived for almost one hundred years alone in the world, her family lost to her before she had any memory of them. But now, she had a brother. Maybe he would share her eye color or the shape of her smile. Perhaps their laughs would be similar or the way they held a pen. Or maybe they'd be as different as chalk and cheese.

She didn't care. They were family. And nothing else mattered.

* * * * *

SPECIAL EXCERPT FROM

HARLEQUIN® *Blaze*®

Ty Slater is a cowboy with a tragic past. And while he's at Thunder Mountain Ranch to celebrate the holidays with his foster family, he meets a woman who might just get past his long-held defenses...

Read on for a sneak preview of A COWBOY UNDER THE MISTLETOE, the first Christmas story in Vicki Lewis Thompson*'s sexy new cowboy saga* ***THUNDER MOUNTAIN BROTHERHOOD.***

They traded the bunched cord back and forth, winding the lights around the branches until Ty looped the end at the top. Then they both stepped back and squinted at the lit Christmas tree to check placement.

"It's almost perfect," Whitney said. "But there's a blank space in the middle."

"I see it." He stepped forward and adjusted one strand lower. Then he backed up. "I think that does it."

"I think so, too."

He heard something in her voice, something soft and yielding that made his heart beat faster. He glanced over at her. She was staring right back at him, her eyes dark and her breathing shallow. If any woman had ever looked more ready to be kissed, he'd eat his hat.

And damned if he could resist her. His gaze locked with hers and his body tightened as he stepped closer. Slowly he combed his fingers through hair that felt as silky as he'd imagined. "We haven't finished with the tree."

"I know." Her voice was husky. "And there's the dancing afterward..."

"We were never going to do that." He pressed his fingertips into her scalp and tilted her head back. "But I think we were always going to do this." And he lowered his head.

She awaited him with lips parted. After the first gentle pressure against her velvet mouth, he sank deeper with a groan of pleasure. So sweet, so damned perfect. She tasted like wine, better than wine, better than anything he could name.

The slide of her arms around his waist sent heat shooting through his veins. As she nestled against him, he took full command of the kiss, swallowing her moan as he thrust his tongue into her mouth.

She welcomed him, slackening her jaw and inviting him to explore. He caught fire, shifting his angle and making love to her mouth until they were both breathing hard and molded together. As he'd known, they fit exactly.

The red haze of lust threatened to wipe out his good intentions, but he caught himself before he slid his hands under her sweater. Gulping for air, he released her and stepped back. Looking into eyes filled with the same need pounding through him nearly had him reaching for her again. "Let's... Maybe we should...back off for a bit."

Love the Harlequin book you just read?

Your opinion matters.

Review this book on your favorite book site, review site, blog or your own social media properties and share your opinion with other readers!

Be sure to connect with us at:
Harlequin.com/Newsletters
Facebook.com/HarlequinBooks
Twitter.com/HarlequinBooks

She walked slowly back to the table and set the bubbling lasagna on a heat-safe pad.

"Maybe I can change your mind," she challenged. The spicy aroma of the Italian food wasn't nearly as tantalizing as the serene smile she flashed. "Like you and Kate and this Stephen fellow are plotting to change this man Digarro's mind about getting his son taken care of."

"That's different. My sister's patient is in more medical danger the longer he's not being treated, and he and his father—"

"Need to understand their limited options?" Lissa's smile deepened at his scowl. "Yes, I heard."

"I've already chosen the option that works best for me," he insisted, forcing himself to listen to his own words while he was at it.

If he'd thought their problems were only about the impotence, he'd have had her flat on her back on the academy's couch despite Stephen Creighton's surprise visit.

"Giving up on you and me isn't an *option,*" Lissa countered. "It's quitting. Look how well that worked for Kate."

"Katie didn't quit," he bit out. He'd let himself believe she had for too long. He couldn't have been more wrong. "She came to Atlanta to avoid being a daily reminder to me that our father beat on our mother for the entire twenty-five years of their marriage. And that Katie had known, and that she hid it to protect me. All those years she knew and never said a word. What does that do to a child?"

"Martin. I—"

"And I guess I knew it, too, in a way. But I pretended everything was sweet Southern pie, right up until I got my hands on my mother's journal and read it all in black and white."

I can't leave without the kids, and I can't support them on my own...

If I can just stop making Jim so angry...

At least if he's hitting me, the kids will be safe....

His mother had resigned herself to a lifetime of abuse for Martin's sake. For Katie's. Jim Rhodes had been an abusive bastard who'd let everyone around him lie to protect his secret.

Martin's entire childhood had been a lie.

"Martin, don't—"

"Don't what!" Now that Lissa was here, now that he was facing what he couldn't bear for her to know, *now* she didn't want to hear it? "After living the way we did, lying the way we did, it's no wonder Katie needed to move to the other side of the state. That her own marriage didn't work.

Do you finally get it? I'm not any more capable of keeping a healthy relationship going than my sister is. My only experience with love was watching my mother be silently tortured every day of my life!"

Lissa should have been shocked. Scared. Running for the door. Instead, she spread her hands on the table and pushed slowly to her feet.

She walked into the family room, trailing her fingers over his mother's favorite Stickley chair, then the miniature rose bush on the table beside it. Lissa had brought it his first week in the hospital. He'd been coaxing the thing to bloom all winter, knowing the flowers would remind him of her.

"So, your world wasn't as happy-go-lucky as you made it out to be," she said. "So, there was a mess—a lot of it. Don't you think maybe I've figured some of that out over the last year? You know, right about the time you were hurt too badly to keep pretending to be everyone's good-time guy?"

Martin nodded. Lissa always had been smarter than people gave her credit for. Smarter and more special than any of the "easy come, easy go" women he'd been with before. Special enough to tempt Oakwood's most determined bachelor to reach out and believe he could hold on to something real.

"So, now you know it all." He made himself stay put instead of going to her and pulling her into his arms. Soothing them both. "It's time for you to head back home to your girls and stop wasting your time chasing something that isn't going to happen with me."

"Tony and Angie said they can watch the girls for a week or so," she replied, talking about her sister and Stephen's ex-chief, who'd been married for years.

"Lissa, look—"

"What makes you think my trip up here is all about you?" she demanded.

"What? So, you've been dying for a vacation to Atlanta, and this is your excuse to get away from it all?"

"Something like that."

"Don't push this, Lissa." He was standing in front of her and didn't remember crossing the room. He reached for her before he could stop himself, cupping her elbow in his hand, rubbing her satin-smooth skin with his thumb.

"Why? Because you're already hard at work pushing yourself?" She gazed around at the memories of home, and her, that he'd dragged all